| WARNING! |
| Major *spoilers* ahead! |

If you have **not finished** reading the core series:

Qualify, Compete, Win, Survive

and the two novellas:

Aeson: Blue and **Aeson: Black**...

It is strongly recommended that you avoid this book!

Mysteries, final relationships, and character fates are revealed (but only within the scope of the original series).

Don't worry, there are no spoilers for the prequel series **Dawn of the Atlantis Grail**.

Calling all valiant Astra Daimon and brilliant Shoelace Girls!

Ready to learn more about your favorite TAG characters? **PEOPLE OF THE ATLANTIS GRAIL** is here to guide you by means of Starlight through the expansive cast of thousands of vibrant and unique souls who populate the universe of *The Atlantis Grail*.

Rediscover beloved characters—real people who reside in your heart as much as they live in your imagination, fill your dreams, and have become your dear friends.

This is our second comprehensive reference book of all things TAG for superfans—that's all of you awesome readers and lovers of TAG! Published in ebook and handsome paper print editions (hardcover and paperback), it's a cornucopia of fun personal facts, nitty-gritty details, new material and revelations about every single character mentioned in the original four-book series—human, alien, and even feline—plus, characters from the two Aeson novellas.

Prepare for fun surprises, such as the introduction of the Atlantean Zodiac, and some *new*, previously unpublished information just for *YOU*!

So, don't be shy, open this exciting collector volume and start exploring!

PEOPLE OF THE ATLANTIS GRAIL *is a part of The Atlantis Grail Superfan Extras series.*

PEOPLE OF THE ATLANTIS GRAIL
Dramatis Personae
A Reference Guide to Characters for Fans of The Atlantis Grail
(The Atlantis Grail Superfan Extras Series)

Vera Nazarian

Cover Design by Vera Nazarian
Cover image elements:
"Sky painting tonight," in Morrillo, Veraguas, Panama, photo by Kate Evans, kateevanswriter.com
"Classical decorative elements in baroque style" by Sdart22, DepositPhotos.
"Earth sunrise with rays and lens flare—Photo" by JohanSwanepoel, DepositPhotos.

FIRST EDITION
Trade Hardcover:
ISBN-13: 978-1-60762-184-3
ISBN-10: 1-60762-184-3

Trade Paperback:
ISBN-13: 978-1-60762-185-0
ISBN-10: 1-60762-185-1

February 21, 2023

A Publication of
Norilana Books
P. O. Box 209
Highgate Center, VT 05459-0209
www.norilana.com

Printed in the United States of America

People of the Atlantis Grail

Dramatis Personae

A Reference Guide to Characters for Fans of The Atlantis Grail

The Atlantis Grail Superfan Extras Series

Norilana Books
Science Fiction

www.norilana.com

Other Books by Vera Nazarian

Lords of Rainbow
Dreams of the Compass Rose
Salt of the Air
The Perpetual Calendar of Inspiration
The Clock King and the Queen of the Hourglass
Mayhem at Grant-Williams High (YA)
The Duke in His Castle
After the Sundial
Mansfield Park and Mummies
Northanger Abbey and Angels and Dragons
Pride and Platypus: Mr. Darcy's Dreadful Secret
Vampires are from Venus, Werewolves are from Mars

Cobweb Bride Trilogy:
Cobweb Bride
Cobweb Empire
Cobweb Forest

The Atlantis Grail:
Qualify (Book One)
Compete (Book Two)
Win (Book Three)
Survive (Book Four)

The Atlantis Grail Novella Series:
Aeson: Blue
Aeson: Black

The Atlantis Grail Superfan Extras Series:
The Atlantis Grail Companion

(Forthcoming)

Dawn of the Atlantis Grail (Prequel Series):
Eos (Book One)
Dea (Book Two)
Niktos (Book Three)
Ghost (Book Four)
Starlight (Book Five)

The Atlantis Grail:
The Book of Everything (Book Five)

Dedication

For the amazing Nancy Huett
without whom this book would have taken forever.

My love and gratitude knows no bounds.

PEOPLE

Of

The Atlantis Grail

Dramatis Personae

A Reference Guide to Characters for Fans of The Atlantis Grail

The Atlantis Grail Superfan Extras Series

VERA NAZARIAN

CONTENTS

Contents

Introduction

Wixameret, TAG Fan! You hold in your hands the ultimate reference to all the characters of *The Atlantis Grail.* . . .

In addition to the comprehensive and all-inclusive ***Dramatis Personae*** section at the end that presents every character ever referenced in the series in alphabetical order with relevant personal information, there are also various sections of character lists.

Major characters are presented up-front in more detail, followed by simple lists of all people (major, secondary, minor, and fleeting) grouped by theme and category. A general pronunciation guide of the Atlantean names is included, in addition to the pronunciations of each individual name. An asterisk * after names indicates characters who never appear on the scene, are deceased, or are ancient historical figures. In addition, certain family members who are never mentioned in the books at all, are included to fill out the family trees, and are referenced only in this fan guide (but may appear in future stories).

There are major *spoilers* aplenty, so if you have not finished reading the core series *(Qualify, Compete, Win, Survive)*, and the two novellas *Aeson: Blue* and *Aeson: Black*, it is strongly recommended that you avoid this book. Mysteries, final relationships, and character fates are revealed (but only within the scope of the original series— don't worry, there are no spoilers for the prequel series ***Dawn of the Atlantis Grail***).

A fun surprise section is the ***Atlantean Zodiac*** which is introduced here, but the astrological personality types and interpretations will be fully covered in their own dedicated volume of ***The Atlantis Grail Superfan Series***.

And now, prepare to take a deep dive into the universe of the fictional but very real people you love!

Pronunciation Guide

The pronunciation of Atlantean names is inspired by many ancient languages including Ancient Egyptian, Ancient Greek, Armenian, Russian, Latin and Romance (Spanish, Italian), plus a sprinkling of other Middle Eastern and Asian linguistic roots.

In general, consonants and vowels are pronounced as written. The vowels "a, e, i, o, u" are pronounced as "ah, eh, ee, oh, oo."

Diphthongs are not common, and most adjacent vowels are pronounced separately, not blended or run together.

Consonants are usually hard. There are no silent letters—everything is pronounced. The letter "h" is pronounced as "kh" (such as "hot"), but the "th" combination is pronounced as in the word "thought." Of course, as with any living, natural language, there are occasional exceptions.

The letter "x" is spoken as "ks" but may be substituted with "z" for ease of pronunciation.

For example, Xelio is pronounced as "KSEH-lee-oh" on Atlantis, but for the English-speaking Earth natives he is "ZEH-lee-oh."

Similarly, Aeson is "Ah-eh-SOHN" on Atlantis, but on Earth he is "AY-sun" or Jason without the "J."

The stress falls on the syllable that is printed in UPPERCASE.

See the ***Dramatis Personae*** section in this book for the correct pronunciation listed directly after each Atlantean character's name.

In addition, the official **YouTube Channel** has several pronunciation videos. Be sure to check it out!

YouTube Channel:
https://www.youtube.com/veranazarian-tag/

Major Characters

The Lark Family

Gwenevere "Gwen" Athena Lark (later, Gwenevere **Kassiopei**)

Role	Main Character, POV Narrator
Eye Color	Blue
Hair Color	Dark Brown
Height	5'9"
Nickname	Shoelace Girl
Family Nickname	Gee Two
Color Quadrant	Yellow
Qualification Semi-Finals Dorm	Yellow Quadrant Dorm Eight
Qualification Finals	Team USA 14C
RQC-3 Rank (out of 6,023)	#4,796
Games of the Atlantis Grail Contender Category / Score	White Vocalist / #6 Champion, 3,972 AG Points
Pilot Call Sign	Lark
Birthdate	May 25, 2030 (Green Amrevet 9, 9757)
Zodiac Sign	Gemini
Home Planet	Earth
Physical Appearance	Tall and slim but with curves, long, wavy dark brown hair, expressive eyes, stooping posture.
Personality Characteristics	Inquisitive, chatty, talkative in classes, hopeful, inspired, uses creative intelligence, dreamer.
Strength	Logos voice, original thinking, bringing people together. Hopeful

	persistence. Motto: "I do not accept [that/this/it]."
Weakness	Physically insecure and awkward, bully victim, fear of heights, know-it-all tendencies, relentlessly argumentative.
Family Members	Father: Charles Lark Mother: Margot Lark Brother (older): George Lark Brother (younger): Gordon Lark Sister (younger): Grace Lark Spouse: Aeson Kassiopei Daughter (1st child): Margot Arlenari Kassiopei Son (2nd child): Romhutat "Rommi" Charles Kassiopei (twin) Son (3rd child): Suval "Suvi" Gordon Kassiopei (twin) Daughter (4th child): Oalla Ann Kassiopei Daughter (5th child): Erita Hasmik Kassiopei
Introduced in	*Qualify*
Appears in	All novels, *Aeson: Black.*

Profile and Facts

Gwen Lark is the main character and first-person narrator of this book series. When the story begins, she is a sixteen-year-old high school junior in Vermont, USA, a self-proclaimed nerd, smart, studious, and creative, but physically awkward and bullied by her peers. In the course of the series, she grows into a confident and powerful young woman, finds true love, reunites her family, and saves two worlds—Earth and Atlantis.

But first, when an asteroid apocalypse threatens Earth, Gwen must Qualify for interplanetary rescue to the colony planet Atlantis, against impossible odds and deadly competition. Saying goodbye to her Classics professor father and former opera diva mother (who is dying from cancer), Gwen is taken to the Qualification compound along with her siblings and other eligible teens. Here she undergoes merciless physical training taught by athletic and intimidating *astra daimon* Atlanteans, and receives *acoustic (sound) technology* training, in preparation for deadly competition in the form of Semi-Finals and Finals. All along, she must also worry about and care for her three siblings, form friendships and alliances, deal with her sexy first crush Logan Sangre, discover another intriguing and complicated relationship, and eventually learn to lead with compassion and a purpose.

Typical of her Yellow Quadrant affiliation, Gwen is curious, inquisitive, creative, and able to think outside the box. Presented with four unique items during a Pre-Qualification personality test (sword, pen, shield, map), she chooses the map, and is assigned to Yellow Quadrant Dorm Eight at the Pennsylvania Regional Qualification Center Three (RQC-3).

Gwen earns the nickname "Shoelace Girl" in a moment of wildly creative thinking. During Combat class, she ends up last, without a practice weapon, and makes her own "weapon" on the spot by pulling out her shoelaces and tying them together to form a cord (Nets and Cords are the Yellow Quadrant weapons), thereby impressing her Atlantean Instructor, Xelio Vekahat.

Gwen also stands up to some of her bullies including Claudia Grito whom she defeats in a sparring match in Combat class. She also befriends the wheelchair-bound Blayne Dubois, whom she later assists in his training in Limited Mobility (LM) Forms Combat.

When Atlantean shuttles crash in a tragic incident of terrorist sabotage, Gwen "sings down" one falling shuttle using a *voice command*, and rescues an enigmatic Atlantean VIP, an injured high-ranking Fleet officer, Aeson Kass. In doing so, she discovers her own rare talent, the Logos voice—an ability to super-focus at the quantum level, and interact directly with the fabric of the universe.

The Logos Voice is a *power voice* recognized by Atlanteans since ancient times. Known as the Voice of Creation, *logos anima mundi*, the "soul of the world," it puts Gwen into a rare category of humans who are able to "perceive" quantum entanglement, negate immense distances, and teleport-travel by means of Starlight. Like the ancient Atlantean princess Arlenari Kassiopei, Gwen is a "Starlight Sorceress."

Gwen keeps her actions a secret, but instead of getting credit for rescuing Aeson Kass, she is instead blamed for the sabotage—until she proves her innocence and reveals her remarkable voice by levitating another shuttle in front of witnesses and Aeson himself (whom she finds insufferable, arrogant, dangerous, and attractive). Kass declares her an important asset for Atlantis and takes charge of her voice training.

After a month of rigorous physical training, Gwen makes some athletic progress, but barely enough. Going into Semi-Finals, she has below-average stats, while her voice earns extraordinary marks:

Achievement Score (AT Score)	Sum: 77 Average: 5.13
Agility	3
Voice	10
Forms	6
Weapons	5
Culture	7
Creativity	7
Intelligence	7
Strength	3
Speed	4
Flexibility	4
Balance	4
Cooperation	6
Assertion	5
Endurance	3
Leadership	3

Ending up in Los Angeles for her Semi-Finals, Gwen and her peers have to run a terrifying obstacle course through the sprawling streets of L.A. toward the city center downtown, and perform outrageous tasks that get many of the teens killed.

Gwen is wounded, commandeers a hoverboard, gains a team of allies, witnesses many deaths, uses her brains and creativity to solve problems, and saves her younger sister Gracie—all before accomplishing the required goals and making it up to one of the Atlantean shuttles waiting in the skies over the city. The last thing Gwen sees before losing consciousness, is Aeson Kass pulling her inside the shuttle.

Gwen wakes up at the National Qualification Center (NQC) in Colorado, her injuries miraculously healed by Atlantean technology, and all three of her siblings at her side, having passed the grueling Semi-Finals.

For those who remain in the running, the training continues. Difficulty is amped up to the next level, and the deadly Finals loom. It is revealed that Gwen's impulsive little sister Gracie made an emotional and foolish error of judgement back at the RQC-3, and was peripherally involved in the shuttle sabotage, so she is about to be Disqualified. However, Gwen intervenes by pleading Gracie's case before Aeson Kass himself, who relents—since Gwen claims he owes her his life—or maybe it is for some other inexplicable reason that Gwen just cannot grasp.

Gracie Lark is reinstated, and everyone focuses on getting those important points. Gwen earns 185 Final Points at NQC, and is assigned to Team USA 14C in the Finals. Teamwork plays a major role in the Finals and, this time around, points and scores are a combination of individual and team efforts.

Just before the Finals, Gwen finds out a shocking secret—Aeson Kass is not merely a high-ranking Fleet officer, but he is, in fact, Aeson Kassiopei, son of the Imperator, member of the ancient Imperial Kassiopei Dynasty, and the Crown Prince of the biggest nation on the colony planet Atlantis.

Gwen's mind is blown, her world turned upside-down, but there is no time to process, only persevere. After a grueling and terrifying hoverboard race through deadly subterranean tunnels and caverns underneath the Atlantic Ocean, from the coast of Florida to the site of the ancient Earth continent Atlantis (somewhere near the Bermuda Triangle), Gwen, her teammates, and siblings, barely escape drowning in the tunnel network, and arrive at the finish line. Their final destination is the immense cavern underneath Ancient Atlantis where they converge together with millions of other Earth teenagers from all across the globe, and from where they have to fly through a volcanic chute up into the sky and waiting shuttles—in order to Qualify.

The four Lark siblings and their peers make a valiant last-second push to the ultimate finish, as an explosion rocks the cavern. At the doors of the waiting shuttle, an Atlantean officer checks their scores, and admits Gwen, Gracie, Gordie, Logan, and many others. Unfortunately, Gwen's older brother George does not Qualify, due to his low team score (most of his team perished).

George puts on a brave front, sings his Shakespearean goodbye, and flies off into the sunset—while his siblings join him in harmony for the Fool's Song. He must remain on the doomed home planet with the rest of the unlucky billions, and die when the doomsday asteroid hits Earth.

With George no longer with them, a sudden burden of additional responsibility for her family falls upon Gwen.

Gwen and the rest of the Qualified are taken on board the 2,000 great Atlantean Fleet ark-ships, commencing their escape toward the colony planet Atlantis and a new life.

The lucky Earth refugees embark on an amazing journey through the solar system and beyond, while the Fleet accelerates into the Quantum Stream (a special force field bubble), in which it will remain for many months until reaching the extreme velocity necessary to make a Jump across the universe to a distant galaxy where the planet Atlantis is located.

In the early days, Gwen and her two remaining siblings start out on Ark-Ship 1109 (AS-1109), until Decision Day when Gwen refuses to choose between becoming a Cadet or a Civilian, stating that she wants to become a Citizen. As a Citizen of Imperial *Atlantida*, Gwen is convinced that she would have the means to rescue the rest of her family on Earth, and obtain access to the high-end medical care that would cure her mother's cancer. But first, in order to earn her Citizenship, Gwen Lark, the awkward klutz, would have to enter the deadly Games of the Atlantis Grail as soon as she arrives on Atlantis. And that's infinitely worse than Qualification.

Because her file was flagged for transfer (on Aeson's direct orders) she is immediately reassigned and transferred to Imperial Command Ship 2 (ICS-2), under the command of Command Pilot Aeson Kassiopei, and appointed to work for him as an Imperial Aide.

In addition, Gwen is given the formal task of being a records keeper for the Central Command Office (CCO), keeping an impartial journal that will serve as a historical record of the journey from Earth to Atlantis.

On ICS-2, she is assigned to the Yellow Quadrant, Navigation and Guidance section. Now that she's an Imperial Aide, instead of living in the barracks or dormitories with other Cadets or Civilians, she is housed in Yellow Quadrant Command Deck Four, Cabin 28.

Aeson, her direct commanding officer, refuses to accept her nonsensical decision of becoming a Citizen, or humor her unrealistic aspirations of entering the Games. He gives her until the end of the journey to make her life choice of becoming a Cadet or Civilian. As a result, Gwen is uniquely permitted to take both Civilian and Cadet classes. Furthermore, as an Imperial Aide, she is also tutored in Imperial Court Protocol so that she can serve the Prince properly, while her private voice lessons from Aeson also continue.

Throughout the ensuing months of the journey, Gwen takes various required classes including shuttle Pilot Training classes and Atlantean Language, Culture, and Technology. At the same time, she works closely with the other two Aides at the CCO, and with Aeson himself. She survives a disturbing hostage situation in which factions of Earth terrorist organization Terra Patria take over and threaten the Atlantean High Command across the four Imperial Command ships, and many Earth refugees are killed before the situation is resolved. That's when she discovers that Aeson Kassiopei is an exemplary commander, an amazing marksman, and a very interesting person— there are so many more layers to his complex personality that she is just starting to fathom.

She also participates in various social and training activities such as the Zero Gravity Dances and Quantum Stream Cadet Pilot Shuttle Races.

Gwen ranks a below-average #547 for her ark-ship at the beginning of the first Cadet Quantum Stream Race, mostly because of her rude and overbearing Pilot Partner Hugo Moreno. During that QS Race, their shuttle Breaches out of the Quantum Stream and into ordinary space in the middle of nowhere (normally a death sentence), but miraculously re-enters the QS when Gwen uses her Logos voice, out of desperation, to key the Quantum Stream to herself.

Their shuttle returns last, and earns a dismal 23% Fleet Score in this first Cadet QS Race, placing their Pilot Pair Score at #624 (in last place of all the Pilot Pairs from their ark-ship), and earning a stern (and oddly emotional) reprimand from Aeson for almost getting killed.

Everyone is permitted to switch partners, so this time Gwen pairs up with a much more compatible Pilot Partner Chiyoko Sato. Gwen ranks #314 at beginning of the second QS Race. This time, their Pilot Pair earns an excellent 96% Fleet Score and ranks #5 for their ark-ship at the end of the Final QS Race.

Never giving up her dream of attaining Citizenship, Gwen enlists the aid of devilishly attractive Atlantean officer Pilot Xelio Vekahat to help her work out and train for the Games of the Atlantis Grail.

Midway through the journey, the Fleet undergoes the Quantum Jump that propels them across the universe into the galactic neighborhood of Atlantis. During this critical time, Gwen undergoes a shocking intimate experience in close quarters with her commanding officer Aeson Kassiopei. It reveals that there is a powerful connection between them, no matter how repressed and forbidden such a thing might be to the Imperial Crown Prince.

As far as social interactions, Gwen continues to be open to people around her. She maintains her friendships with Laronda Aimes, Dawn Williams, Hasmik Tigranian, Blayne Dubois and others. She also experiences a breakup with Logan Sangre (her first boyfriend) during the Blue Zero-G Dance where, for the first time, Gwen realizes she might indeed have intense feelings for someone else—Aeson Kassiopei. The time has come to be honest with herself.

Emotionally sunk, Gwen does not attend the Green Zero-G Dance. However, she goes to the Red Zero-G Dance as Xelio Vekahat's date, even while her mind is set on Aeson. In order to make an impression on Kassiopei, Gwen chooses the perfect red dress and enlists the aid of her Court Protocol Instructor Consul Denu and his assistant Kem to help her with her hair and makeup. Attired as the seductress Carmen during the Red Zero-G Dance, Gwen sings the *Habanera* from the opera, directing all her passion at one man, and makes certain that Aeson Kassiopei sees her as a woman. In that moment it becomes clear the Prince desires her, but he remains bound by duty. Outwardly, nothing changes between them—he maintains his distance, and their working relationship continues as before.

During the Yellow Zero G-Dance, Gwen and Aeson dance together in a bittersweet romantic gesture of final parting, and certain emotional truths are revealed.

Soon after, however, Aeson Kassiopei breaks Gwen's heart, coldly informing her that there can be nothing between them once they arrive on Atlantis.

Immediately upon landing, by order of the Imperator, Gwen has to make herself presentable and attend the Imperial Court Assembly. There, in an impossible moment of shocking wonder, Aeson Kassiopei chooses her as his Imperial Bride and Consort, against the wishes of his Father, before the entire Imperial Court.

Now that Gwen is the Bride of the Imperial Crown Prince, with the honorific title of "Imperial Lady" and various privileges, it would seem that her future is bright, since she will automatically become a Citizen upon marriage, and her wishes on behalf of her Earth family will be granted. But Gwen has to deal with a malicious and terrifying future Father-in-Law—the Imperator himself.

Romhutat Kassiopei punishes his son Aeson in the most exquisite manner imaginable—by ensuring that his Bride becomes a Contender in the annual Games of the Atlantis Grail. This death sentence comes in the guise of a favor—an Imperial Gift to the Bride by the Imperator during a celebratory Court Ceremony.

Unable to refuse the Imperial "favor," Gwen officially enters the Games in the Vocalist Category. But first she receives a crash course—the best physical training, incredible support, and advice—from many experts, friends, and loved ones, with Aeson resolved to keep his beloved safe.

The Games happen, like a whirlwind nightmare, with Four Stages of mounting difficulty and unbelievable obstacles and tasks—while Aeson is forced by his cruel Imperial Father to watch every moment of it (and he does, literally, not sleeping for days).

At first the Imperial Bride is universally mocked. Everyone bets against her, and she even becomes the first Contender to be "awarded" the dubious honor of Audience Top Choice for a "Favorite Kill."

But then, slowly, something changes, and her genuine personality emerges under the harsh scrutiny of the public. Somehow, Gwen not only survives, but forms her own loyal Team Lark, attracting many worthy Contender teammates—such as the intriguing and unpredictable Brie Walton, who has been planted in the Games by Aeson in order to help Gwen. This is where Gwen's leadership skills finally shine—quiet, unassuming, and compassionate. And then her vocalist abilities come out, impressing the audience and all of Atlantis.

Gwen manages to survive without killing anyone, for the vast majority of the Games. She uses her wits, her creativity, and sometimes her own ridiculous shortcomings to get things done—such as accidentally pulling down the pants of a dangerous Contender during a mass skirmish.

In Red Stage One, Gwen amazingly escapes being slaughtered in the arena, and starts to make personal connections with other Contenders, as well as gain the attention of dangerous enemies.

During Blue Stage Two, forced to climb the random levitating blocks of the Great Pyramid of Giza (brought to Atlantis as part of the Earth Mission), Gwen hallucinates seeing Ancient Egyptian gods, her brothers, her parents, and Aeson. Are these merely drug-induced visions or something more? The vision of her mother, in particular, seems to be meaningful.

In Green Stage Three, Gwen and Team Lark have to cross concentric hell-circles of ocean and land, while fighting off other treacherous Contenders and discovering their personal limits of endurance.

And in the final stage, Yellow Stage Four, Gwen not only wins the deadly Triathlon Race (and hence, Stage Four), but makes a profound connection to an amazing alien life form, the *pegasei*, who figure strongly in the fateful events to come.

During a final tie-breaker event at the grand stadium, Gwen uses her Logos voice to perform what she thinks is a dramatic feat of levitation, by raising the ancient national monument of the Atlantis Grail. Instead, she unearths more than she bargained for—an ancient secret that sets the final events in motion.

At this point it becomes evident that Gwen is a powerful player in the political sense as well, and a worthy future Imperatris.

The Imperator grudgingly relents, and Gwen officially earns her Atlantis Citizenship by becoming Top Ten Champion #6 and the winner of the Vocalist Category.

She is the Imperial Bride of Aeson Kassiopei, "Shoelace Girl," Grail Games Champion, Logos voice wielder, "Gebi Goddess," and a force to be reckoned with. In the process of her final act in the Games, Gwen has unwittingly broken an ancient Quantum Shield that has held various cosmic elements together for thousands of years since Atlanteans arrived on the colony planet.

And now the unearthed ancient ark-ship Vimana (whose top portion is none other than the Atlantis Grail "monument") is once more broadcasting a signal across the universe. The ancient alien enemy is on its way, and humanity everywhere is in danger.

In addition, a family tragedy befalls, as Gwen discovers that her sick mother has died back on Earth, due to a delay in being rescued and given Atlantean medical care—the result of malicious orders from the Imperator and the conflicted loyalties of *astra daimon* Nefir Mekei. At least George and her father are saved and on their way to Atlantis.

As the alien threat grows, and a mysterious Ghost Moon appears in the skies, the Imperial Wedding is scheduled, and Gwen and Aeson reunite to undergo rigorous traditional preparations.

In a magnanimous act of generosity, Gwen grants Champion Wishes to her teammates and even former adversaries—Chihar, Lolu, Tuar, Sofia, and Fawzi, and a posthumous one to Zaap.

Many subtle changes are brewing, all thanks to Gwen. Her humane addendum to the rules of the brutal Games, establishes a new kind of prize—high points awarded to Contenders who complete each game stage but kill the fewest people.

Gwen and Aeson prepare for their grand Wedding, at the same time as they secretly work with the Imperator to try to control the various components of the damaged Quantum Shield—the Ghost Moon, the ark-ship Vimana, the Ra Disk in New Deshret, and the Rim of the black hole Ae-Leiterra (where Aeson once died, was resurrected by the benevolent *pegasei*, and became the black-armband wearing hero of Atlantis).

The alien enemy arrives at last, in the form of golden light sphere-ships, and starts destroying various outposts and space stations around the Helios system, while Earth reports a similar threat forming. Alien war is imminent, but the enemy appears invulnerable, even as the international fleets and the Star Pilot Corps mobilize, with Aeson Kassiopei in command of them all.

The Earth Larks arrive on Atlantis in time for the Wedding rehearsal dinner. The two families meet and tense moments happen, in addition to revelations that both Charles Lark and Gordie Lark have the Logos voice.

Gwen and the others explore the subterranean mysteries of the ancient ship Vimana, and discover interesting ancient artifacts that reveal the writings of an ancient scribe Semmi, and a note from an even more mysterious ancient named Arleana, Starlight Sorceress.

The Imperial Wedding happens, with grandeur and heart-tugging moments of joy, as Gwen and Aeson marry on Red Amrevet 9, 9771, with family and friends at their side, then unite as lovers at last on their Amrevet Night.

But there is no time to rest, as more space outposts are destroyed. Six Logos voices join during the first *astroctadra* mission, and the Ghost Moon (the secret fourth moon of Atlantis) is brought out of its incorporeal quantum state into real space. An ancient ship graveyard is discovered on its surface, together with a missing Vimana Habitat that houses a mysterious ancient sarcophagus.

Inside the sarcophagus, encased in a jewel, they find the miraculously preserved body of an ancient princess, Arlenari Kassiopei. She is an Imperial ancestor who has been erased from history, and is none other than Arleana, Starlight Sorceress. Her diary, The Book of Everything, reveals great mysteries, including the truth about *pegasei*, the nature of Starlight, and a means to defeat the alien enemy once and for all.

The Imperator meets with other foreign heads of state, and the *pegasei* are revealed as sentient beings who must be set free. Gwen teaches everyone how to communicate with them using a special frequency, and leads one of the *Pegasei* Retrieval Missions with a special forces team to free the remaining *pegasei*.

Together with the sarcophagus of Arlenari, the *pegasei* must pass through the wormhole at Ae-Leiterra, and be returned to Earth, in order to properly seal the deadly quantum rift on Earth. The rift, improperly created by ignorant humans, was the reason for the alien enemy's original asteroid destruction of ancient Atlantis.

Romhutat Kassiopei takes it upon himself to conduct the *pegasei* and Arlenari to the Rim of the black hole, in a self-sacrificing mission that almost redeems him. He also abdicates his Throne, making Aeson the new Archaeon Imperator, and Gwen the Archaeona Imperatris.

Everyone embarks on the second, even greater *astroctadra* mission, this time to protect the whole planetary system by creating an immense Quantum Shield around the star Helios and contain the alien enemy golden spheres. Before departure, they hold a farewell Green Zero-G Dance, and say their emotional goodbyes.

During the final mission, two of their ships explode, and Gwen and several companions including Erita, Hasmik, Xelio, George, Manala and others are marooned in space, some of them floating in their spacesuits.

Before help comes, Gwen manages to organize an amazing and inspired long-distance rescue of Earth from the asteroid strike, communicating through nothing but interstellar equipment, coordinating individuals across immense cosmic distances, as she and others with Logos voices and all of Earth sing together. This places Earth in a temporary quantum bubble while the asteroid passes through it harmlessly.

With oxygen running out, Erita gives her life for Gwen, while Hasmik sacrifices herself for a whole ship of people including Xelio, Manala, George, and Consul Denu. Gwen desperately calls upon the *pegasei* for help, and they keep the two heroic women alive until rescue comes.

Just before disappearing forever, Arion, the alien *pegasus* entity, gives Gwen enough to think about so that she can fathom the elusive nature of Starlight. And it's just in time, because Gwen needs to use Starlight to bring Aeson to her and complete the rescue of Erita and Hasmik.

She also needs it in order to convince the alien enemy, in the form of ancient gods Thoth, Set, Isis, and Horus, to stop the destruction of humanity.

Now that Gwen can use Starlight and correctly open dimensional rifts, she can take a breath and simply be Gwen. Not a goddess, not a sorceress, but a bright young human who has her beloved, her family, her friends, and two worlds to nurture, and safely bring forth a new generation.

George Nestor Lark

Role	Gwen's Older Brother
Eye Color	Blue
Hair Color	Dark Brown
Height	6'0"
Family Nickname	Gee One
Color Quadrant	Green
Qualification Semi-Finals Dorm	Green Quadrant Dorm Eleven
Qualification Finals	Team USA 14B
RQC-3 Rank (out of 6,023)	#3,298
Birthdate	July 24, 2029 (Red Pegasus 25, 9756)
Zodiac Sign	Leo
Home Planet	Earth
Physical Appearance	Tall, medium built, attractive and pleasant looking, average athletic.
Personality Characteristics	Friendly, sarcastic, popular and charming, with a good sense of style and witty humor, loyal and dependable.
Strength	Taking care of people that he loves. Resilience.
Weakness	Relies on sarcasm, does not always express his true feelings. Does not have firm goals.
Family Members	Father: Charles Lark Mother: Margot Lark Sister (younger): Gwen Lark Brother (younger): Gordon Lark Sister (youngest): Grace Lark

Introduced in	*Qualify*
Appears in	*Qualify*, *Compete* (mentioned), *Win* (mentioned), *Survive*.

Profile and Facts

George Lark is Gwen's older brother and is seventeen years old at the beginning of the story. He is a senior at Mapleroad Jackson High School, a popular boy who has many friends and acquaintances, and initially prefers not to hang out with his younger and "less cool" siblings. When the Qualification process begins however, he takes immediate responsibility, and begins to look after the other Larks.

At the RQC-3 compound, George is assigned to the Green Quadrant, although he never admits to picking the shield during the initial test (it's a safe assumption). He is housed at Green Dorm Eleven.

George is not particularly athletic, and does not really stand out in any of his classes. However, he is there to help his sister Gwen when she is falsely accused of sabotage and arrested. George goes to the jail facility in the compound, accompanied by his younger brother Gordie and a minor crowd of others, Candidates who care about Gwen and are determined to do something on her behalf.

At the RQC-3, George briefly and informally dates Amy Calver, a fellow Candidate.

Going into the Semi-Finals, he ranks at #3,298 at the RQC-3, and picks New York for his competition arena.

For the Finals, George earns 179 points (plus an additional unspecified number of final points that qualifies him for Team B) at the NQC, and is assigned to Team USA 14B, a better rank and team placement than Gwen. However, because the majority of his teammates perish in one of the dangerous subterranean caverns during the tunnel race, decimating their team average score, it brings down his cumulative score (a combination of personal and team scores). As a result, he does not Qualify.

George realizes this in advance, but continues in the race, all the way to the bitter end, in order to help his siblings however he can. He makes sure they get on the Atlantean shuttles, and then sings the fool's song, also known as "Feste's Song," from Shakespeare's *Twelfth Night*, as he flies away on his hoverboard. This song was something the Lark family sang together with their mother when they were younger, and George uses it to say goodbye, and allow his siblings to sing with him one last time, in a bittersweet moment of parting.

While Gwen, Gordie, and Gracie continue onward with the Atlanteans, George returns home to be with their parents and wait for the doomsday asteroid to strike.

Although Gwen experiences a hallucination of George in the Great Pyramid during the games in *Win*, the story does not return to George until he is being rescued from apocalyptic Earth, alongside his father, Charles Lark, and the burial urn of his deceased mother, Margot Lark, in *Survive*.

Initially, George and his father end up on board Ark-Ship 1999, the last remaining Fleet ark-ship secretly orbiting Earth. Pedantic Imperial loyalist Nefir Mekei artificially delays their family rescue for days and weeks, upon the Imperator's cruel orders, until Margot succumbs to the cancer, and only then do they finally get picked up.

From there, upon Aeson's direct orders, George and Charles are relegated to the care of Quoni Enutat, one of the more reliable *astra daimon*. They take a high-velocity smaller ship, a velo-cruiser, with Quoni piloting (together with a small crew), and arrive in Atlantis just in time, a few days before the Imperial Wedding.

Unlike all the regular Earth refugees before him, George has missed a whole year of Fleet classes and competition, is behind the others in terms of Atlantean experience, and has no idea what to do with himself in this strange, new, alien environment.

When meeting the Imperial Family, he refuses to be intimidated by the Imperator, and his sarcastic confidence shines through. Since the beginning, George has never been a particular fan of Atlanteans, not trusting their intentions, and even going so far as to call them the derogatory term "Goldilocks" back on Earth. And now that he's here, George is still not trusting, still bitter and cynical.

When the young Imperial Princess Manala loses her runaway cat Khemji and suffers an emotional breakdown, George is the only person who does not accept her tantrum and doles out some no-nonsense, harsh words, making a terrible impression on her. Later however, overcoming his childhood fear of cats, George redeems himself in Manala's eyes, by finding Khemji, and bringing him back to the Palace—all while getting terribly scratched up in the process.

George also accompanies Manala on both the *Astroctadra* Missions, and asks her to dance at the Green Zero-G Dance when no one else would.

In the end, George still has not made a career choice, but Consul Denu seems to think he would make an excellent diplomat.

Gordon "Gordie" Perseus Lark

Role	Gwen's Younger Brother
Eye Color	Blue
Hair Color	Light Brown/Dirty Blond
Height	6'2"
Nickname	Gordie
Family Nickname	Gee Three
Color Quadrant	Blue
Qualification Semi-Finals Dorm	Blue Quadrant Dorm Two
Qualification Finals	Team USA 14A
RQC-3 Rank (out of 6,023)	#1,941
Birthdate	February 7, 2033 (Green Mar-Yan 2, 9759)
Zodiac Sign	Aquarius
Home Planet	Earth
Physical Appearance	Tall after growth spurt, average built, nerdy looking, unathletic, wears rimless glasses. Short buzz-cut hair.
Personality Characteristics	Asocial loner, artistic, listens to music and draws, super-focused and fearless, intelligent, enjoys the unusual, a wild card.
Strength	Creative and artistic, sharp-shooter, organized, has the Logos voice, is open to new experiences.
Weakness	Highly withdrawn, low social skills, bully victim, neglects himself and his appearance, insecure, does not believe he will survive or Qualify.

Family Members	Father: Charles Lark Mother: Margot Lark Brother (oldest): George Lark Sister (older): Gwen Lark Sister (youngest): Grace Lark
Introduced in	*Qualify*
Appears in	All novels.

Profile and Facts

Gordie Lark is Gwen's younger brother, a fourteen-year-old high school freshman at the beginning of the story. Nerdy and introspective, single-mindedly focused on his art and music, he is highly intelligent and observant of fine detail. His clothing is often paint-stained and his rimless glasses are smudged.

Gordie makes it through Pre-Qualification along with his siblings, and admits to having chosen a pen during the initial Quadrant test. This puts him in the Blue Quadrant Dorm Two at the RQC-3.

During Qualification training, Gordie does really well and earns more points than his siblings. He excels in marksmanship, and he seems to enjoy the hoverboard. Even though he's not athletic, he is in some ways fearless, which helps him to achieve more than average. Gordie has a childish sense of wonder about many things, and loves to learn and experience the world to the fullest. This includes his love of food and eating heaping plates of whatever is being served.

Early during training, Gordie gets into a fight where a bully gives him a face bruise and black eye.

Going into the Semi-Finals, he ranks #1,941 at RQC-3, and chooses New York for his competition arena where he gets mildly wounded, grazed by a bullet and his face cut up by knives, but survives, and is completely healed by Atlantean high tech medical care at the NQC.

For the Finals, Gordie earns 216 Final Points at the NQC, and gives 60 points to their youngest sister Gracie in order to help and raise her score. He is assigned to Team USA 14A, and Qualifies.

Gordie is transported via shuttle to Ark-Ship 1109 where he stays for the whole journey to Atlantis. During Decision Day, he chooses Civilian as his life choice, is assigned to Network Systems, and resides in the residential dorm of Blue Quadrant Residential Deck Two.

Throughout the journey, he spends a lot of time working at the Hydroponics Deck, where he also draws plants and watches a girl on whom he has a crush, from afar. He also enjoys the experience of zero gravity dancing.

When they arrive on Atlantis, Gordie gets his Civilian job placement in Poseidon and ends up working in cultivation and crops production design tech at Heri Agriculture, where he gets to design crop planting patterns (horizontal and vertical, for planting in soil, air, and water), and where the employee food court serves delicious *ecurami*.

Gordie supports his sister Gwen in her difficult new role, watches her survive and win the Games of the Atlantis Grail, and grows up in every sense of the word. When the Lark Family is reunited on Atlantis, and Gordie stands next to his older brother for the first time after being separated for over a year, he is now taller than George.

In addition, when Gordie gets tested along with everyone else in the Lark family, upon the Imperator's orders, he has the Logos voice.

Gordie ends up assigned to both the *Astroctadra* Missions. During the Ghost Moon mission, he is sent to the moon Pegasus with Erita Qwas in charge. Afterwards, they fly to the surface of the newly materialized fourth moon of Atlantis, where Gordie, along with others, explores the ancient ship graveyard and the Habitat from Vimana. When the sarcophagus of Arlenari is discovered, Gordie is the one who notices the miniature scrolls of The Book of Everything hidden inside the clear jewels.

For the Helios system grand *astroctadra* mission, Gordie is assigned on board War-8 under the command of Lafaoh Ungreb of Bastet and sent to the Tammuz coordinate point. Accompanying him is Oalla Keigeri and his father Charles Lark with the urn of Margot Lark.

During the Green Zero G-Dance on the eve of the mission, Gordie is asked to dance by a male *astra daimon* Nergal Duha, and he is open-minded and happy to oblige, regardless of gender or sexual orientation.

Grace "Gracie" Hera Lark

Role	Gwen's Younger Sister
Eye Color	Blue
Hair Color	Dirty Blond
Height	5'6"
Nickname	Gracie, Lark Two (by Blayne)
Family Nickname	Gee Four
Color Quadrant	Red
Qualification Semi-Finals Dorm	Red Quadrant Dorm Five
Qualification Finals	Team USA 14D
RQC-3 Rank (out of 6,023)	#4,482
Birthdate	August 14, 2034 (Red Amrevet 25, 9760)
Zodiac Sign	Leo
Home Planet	Earth
Physical Appearance	Slightly taller than average, skinny and young, long hair.
Personality Characteristics	Risk-taking, brave, impulsive, pushy, with a good sense of style.
Strength	Gutsy, courageous, aggressive in going after what she wants.
Weakness	Immature, prone to being childish, far too impulsive.
Family Members	Father: Charles Lark Mother: Margot Lark Brother (oldest) George Lark Sister (older): Gwen Lark Brother (older): Gordon Lark
Introduced in	*Qualify*
Appears in	All novels, *Aeson: Black* (mention).

Profile and Facts

Grace Lark is Gwen's younger sister and youngest sibling. When the story begins, she is twelve years old, a seventh grader at Mapleroad Jackson Middle School, and barely eligible for Qualification. Gracie is still very immature and going through a whiny stage.

During the initial Pre-Qualification testing, Gracie picks the knife, and is then assigned to Red Quadrant Dorm Five at the RQC-3. She passes the Pre-Qualification hoverboard test after being inspired by the exemplary efforts of the boy in the wheelchair whom she later meets as Blayne Dubois.

At the RQC compound, Gracie immediately finds her courage, embraces her Red Quadrant side, and develops a crush on a much older boy, Daniel Tover. In an attempt to impress him, she gets marginally involved with an Earth terrorist group responsible for the shuttle sabotage incident, and hides a stolen navigation chip in Laronda Aimes' pocket, effectively framing her.

Going into the Semi-Finals, Gracie ranks at #4,482 at the RQC-3, and picks Los Angeles as her competition arena. She barely survives the ordeal with her sister Gwen's help, and ends up at the NQC. There, her role in the sabotage is revealed and she is disqualified by the Atlantis Central Agency (ACA) for secondary involvement with shuttle incident. After Gwen pleads her case, she is reinstated by Aeson Kass and given a blank slate of zero points.

For the Finals, Gracie earns 70 Points at the NQC, and receives an additional 60 points from her brother Gordie to give her a fighting chance.

She is assigned to Team USA 14D in the Finals, and eventually Qualifies, but not without help from Gwen, followed by a last-minute save from Blayne Dubois who catches her with the Grip of Friendship as she falls from her hoverboard.

Once Qualified, Gracie is transported via shuttle to Ark-Ship 1109, on which she remains for the entirety of the journey to Atlantis. On Decision Day, she chooses Fleet Cadet as her life choice, and is assigned to the Red Quadrant, Drive and Propulsion, and resides in the barracks on Cadet Deck One.

Gracie also starts dating Blayne Dubois, especially after their time together at the Blue Zero-G Dance.

Gracie earns a 78% Fleet Score at end of the first Cadet Quantum Steam Race. She then earns a 90% Fleet Score, and her Pilot Pair ranks #35 for their ark-ship at end of the second and Final QS Race.

Once on Atlantis, Gracie divides her time between her Fleet Cadet duties and helping out Gwen with her role, and supporting her in the Games. When the notification comes that their mother, Margot Lark, has passed away during Games Stage Two, Gracie tells Aeson not to let Gwen know, so as not to throw her off her focus. When the Games are over and Gwen is told, Gracie takes full responsibility for this well-intended deception and then acts like an older sister, helping Gwen recuperate and deal with the aftermath.

When Gracie watches the private farewell video left to her by their mother, she takes to heart the meaning of her middle name, "Hera," and Margot's words of wisdom that she is a warrior already, but needs to remember that she is a queen.

When the alien war begins, Gracie is deployed with the Imperial Fleet, and is assigned to War-1 with the other Fleet Cadets, to stay in orbit over their new home planet itself and defend Atlantis.

She and Blayne dance together at the Green Zero-G Dance, along with everyone else. Then, after the enemy golden spheres are neutralized, she has stories to tell of their piloting skills and aerial defense of Atlantis.

Charles Lark

Role	Gwen's Father, Professor of Classics and History (University of Vermont)
Eye Color	Blue
Hair Color	Light Brown, with Grey
Height	5'11"
Color Quadrant	Blue
Birthdate	December 7, 1995 (Green Ghost Moon 1, 9730)
Zodiac Sign	Sagittarius
Home Planet	Earth
Physical Appearance	Average, medium built, wavy tousled brown hair greying at the temples, rimless glasses.
Personality Characteristics	Epitome of academia, quietly introspective, intellectual, gentle-spoken, eccentric, living inside his head and historical research. Loves his wife and children deeply.
Strength	Intellectual, analytical, highly educated, gentle, open-minded, filled with wonder, inspired by and expert in antiquity. Has the Logos voice.
Weakness	Broken by the death of his wife, quietly depressed, absentminded, forgetful, health undermined by Atlantean heavy gravity.
Family Members	Father: Graham Lark (deceased) Mother: Flavia Lark née Nucci (deceased) Spouse: Margot Lark Son (1st child): George Lark Daughter (2nd child): Gwenevere Lark Son (3rd child): Gordon Lark Daughter (4th child): Grace Lark
Introduced in	*Qualify*
Appears in	All novels.

Profile and Facts

Charles Lark, Gwen's father, is a Professor of Classics and History at the University of Vermont. He takes this position in order to move the family from California, after his wife Margot gets cancer from the coastal radiation.

Charles is the epitome of the absentminded professor, intelligent, and steeped in antiquity. He loves to tell his children stories and trivia about classical subjects, and he is responsible for the Greek Gods and Heroes middle names of all his children (they don't talk about it).

Although he was not tested for it, Charles is aligned with the Blue Quadrant based on his personality.

Because of his daughter Gwen's relationship with Aeson, member of the Imperial Family on Atlantida, Charles is rescued from Earth alongside his son, George. Unfortunately, his terminally ill wife Margot dies before she could be helped by Atlantean high-tech medicine, so Charles brings the urn with her remains with him to Atlantis.

Charles is transported up to Ark-Ship 1999, orbiting in stealth over Earth, then taken directly to Atlantis on a high velocity cruiser piloted by Quoni Enutat and a small crew, arriving in time for his daughter Gwen's Imperial Wedding.

Landing on Atlantis, Charles immediately suffers the effects of high gravity and is very ill for several days, having to be medicated until he acclimates to the new planetary environment.

Charles meets the rest of the in-laws, the Imperial Kassiopei Family during a tense and terrible *dea* meal equivalent of a "rehearsal dinner," and resists the Imperator's *compelling voice*, which gets him noticed. He finds a sympathetic friend in Imperatris Devora, who instinctively understands the depth of his loss and the burden of grief.

Then, during an emotionally grueling voice test ordered by the Imperator, Charles reveals that he has the Logos voice. However, he is much too heartbroken, tired, and unwell to use it properly, so he does not actively participate in any of the *astroctadra* missions, although he does accompany his son Gordie on the final Helios mission, taking Margot's urn with him.

Charles is instrumental in discovering The Book of Everything on the sarcophagus of Arlenari, by noticing certain cartouches and making other expert observations.

After the alien war is over, Charles takes Margot's urn and scatters her ashes over a beautiful waterfall at Aeson's favorite Kassiopei Family estate, while his children watch. Now that Margot, the love of his life, is on Atlantis permanently, Charles says he can never leave. "Atlantis is home."

Charles accepts a position in the newly opened Earth antiquities wing of the Imperial Poseidon Museum, as an Earth historian, where he works on research, lectures, and teaches.

Margot Lark

Role	Gwen's Mother, Former Opera Singer
Eye Color	Blue
Hair Color	Dark Brown, then bald due to hair loss from chemotherapy.
Height	5'7"
Color Quadrant	Red
Birthdate	October 17, 2000 (Blue Ghost Moon 16, 9733)
Zodiac Sign	Libra
Home Planet	Earth
Physical Appearance	Average build, charismatically attractive and elegant, with curves, painfully thin toward the end due to cancer.
Personality Characteristics	Warm and loving, playful, powerful on-stage presence and operatic voice, a good sense of style, outgoing.
Strength	Strong and indomitable, beautiful mezzo soprano operatic voice, a loving mother, charming, a tough and stubborn fighter.
Weakness	Loves too much, can be somewhat overbearing.
Family Members	Father: Albert Walden (estranged) Mother: Clarabeth Walden née Junge (estranged) Sister: Eugenia Walden Spouse: Charles Lark Son (1st child): George Lark Daughter (2nd child): Gwenevere Lark Son (3rd child): Gordon Lark Daughter (4th child): Grace Lark
Introduced in	*Qualify*
Appears in	All novels.

Profile and Facts

Margot Lark née Walden is Gwen's mother, and a former opera singer. She has to stop working once she develops lung cancer, due to the coastal radiation, when they live in California. As a result, the whole family relocates to Vermont where her husband Charles accepts a teaching position at UVM.

Margot has a beautiful mezzo soprano voice, and once had an impressive operatic career, singing at the Met and other venues.

Although she was not tested for it, Margot is aligned with the Red Quadrant based on her personality.

Margot stubbornly keeps living and fights to stay alive, long after three of her children Qualify and are taken away to Atlantis.

However, after a very difficult year on Earth, lack of resources, scarcity of medical supplies, and other horrors of the apocalyptic Earth, Margo succumbs to the cancer. She dies on Earth the day before the family is rescued and taken up to the ark ship. She is soon cremated on board Ark-Ship 1999 and her ashes brought in an urn to Atlantis.

Before she dies, Margot records farewell videos for each of her children. Gwen gets to see her video on her Fasting and Cleansing Day, just before the Wedding. In the video, Margot reveals that she is aware of Aeson and Gwen's relationship and the upcoming Wedding. It is not mentioned how she knows, but it can be safely assumed that during their many awkward communications with Nefir Mekei, as he told his various lies to stall their rescue, he managed to let it slip that there is an Imperial Wedding, and that Gwen and Aeson were getting married.

In the end of the video, Margot tells Gwen that she loves her "to Atlantis and back." These are the exact same words that Gwen heard in a drug-induced hallucination during Blue Stage Two of the Games when she was in the Great Pyramid of Giza and saw a vision of her parents. There is a very strong likelihood that this vision of Margot happened at the *very same moment* when Margot died back on Earth. And when the vision tells Gwen to run, it literally saves her life.

In Gracie's video Margot tells her daughters that Gracie is a warrior already, but needs to remember that she is a queen, while Gwen knows she is a queen already but needs to remember that she is a warrior.

After the alien war is over, Charles takes Margot's urn and scatters her ashes over a beautiful waterfall at Aeson's favorite Kassiopei Family estate, while their children watch. A flock of birds rises, and in the watery mist and rainbows, just for a moment, Margot flies.

The Imperial Kassiopei Family

Aeson "Kass" Kassiopei

Role	Imperial Crown Prince of *Atlantida*, SPC Commander, ICS-2 Command Pilot, Gwen's Soul Mate and Husband
Eye Color	Lapis Lazuli Blue
Hair Color	Golden
Height	6'4"
Nickname	Kass
Color Quadrant	Blue, but wears Black Armband of Honor
Pilot Call Sign	Phoebos
SPC Pilot Special Affiliation	*Astra Daimon*
Birthdate	Blue Amrevet 21, 9751 (September 9, 2023)
Zodiac Sign	Radiant Kheprio (Scarab)
Home Planet	Atlantis
Physical Appearance	Tall and lean, light bronze skin, perfectly toned, exquisitely handsome, with chiseled features, dark brows and *wedjat* eyes (natural dark pigment "lined" eyelids), and long golden hair of the Kassiopei Dynasty.
Personality Characteristics	Reserved, commanding presence, highly controlled, sly, intelligent, orderly, dutiful, intensely focused.
Strength	Just and fiercely loving, benevolent natural leader. Top solo pilot, top marksman sharp-shooter. Has the Logos voice. Skilled at deception.

Weakness	Overly protective, pedantic tendencies, overly dutiful, conflicted, resorts to lying when confronted.
Family Members	Father: Romhutat Kassiopei, Archaeon Imperator of *Atlantida* Mother: Devora Kassiopei, Archaeona Imperatris of *Atlantida* Sister (younger): Manala Kassiopei, Imperial Princess Spouse: Gwen Lark Daughter (1st child): Margot Arlenari Kassiopei Son (2nd child): Romhutat "Rommi" Charles Kassiopei (twin) Son (3rd child): Suval "Suvi" Gordon Kassiopei (twin) Daughter (4th child): Oalla Ann Kassiopei Daughter (5th child): Erita Hasmik Kassiopei Six other anonymous children.
Introduced in	*Qualify*
Appears in	All novels, *Aeson: Blue, Aeson: Black.*

Profile and Facts

Aeson Kassiopei (AY-SUN KASS [Earth] / AH-EH-SOHN KAH-SEE-OH-PAY [Atlantis]), Imperial Crown Prince and Heir of Imperial *Atlantida*, is Gwen Lark's ultimate romantic interest, her soul mate and love. Before they are joined together, both have to understand themselves and each other, and conquer many internal and external obstacles.

Aeson is approximately twenty-three Earth years old (eighteen Atlantean years) when he first meets Gwen in 2047.

As the sole Heir to the most powerful and original nation on the colony planet Atlantis, Aeson bears a world of responsibilities on his shoulders. His relationship with his cruel, unpredictable, and tyrannical father, Romhutat, has shaped his personality since earliest childhood. Aeson has learned to repress all emotions, conceal his true opinions, and strive to please his Imperial Father's capricious whims.

Aeson cannot be compelled by his father's *compelling voice* but the one time he stood up to him, the Imperator punished others he cared about. As a result, Aeson goes along with the compulsions and pretends to submit.

His mother, Devora, is a powerful loving force, who, together with his younger sister Manala provide the much-needed warmth and affection to offset the cold cruelty of his father.

As a young boy, Aeson convinces his parents to permit him to attend Fleet Cadet School where he graduates near the top of his class as an Imperial Fleet Pilot along with others his own age. Intelligent, detail-oriented, and studious, he aligns with the Blue Quadrant. Soon, Aeson discovers he is an excellent Pilot and precision marksman (top of his class), and aspires to join the international Star Pilot Corps and even become one of the *astra daimon*.

Aeson makes complex lifelong friendships, learns to get along with difficult people, and experiences his first crush on fellow student Elikara Vekahat who dies soon after graduation on her first mission on behalf of the Imperator.

Devastated by the loss, Aeson punishes himself by denying himself the pursuit of his original career trajectory. He pulls himself back, retreats inward, and remains as an ordinary Imperial Fleet Pilot, even while his friends go on to join the SPC and become *astra daimon*.

However, soon after, he is sent on a regular maintenance mission along with his Imperial Father to the Rim of the giant black hole Ae-Leiterra to maintain the Great Quantum Shield. Here, in a critical moment, during a disastrous turn of events when the Imperator hesitates to perform his suicide mission duty, Aeson does it for him.

Aeson flies his shuttle outside the safety barrier in order to extend and reinforce it and saves the Fleet, while he and his shuttle are crushed and incinerated by the forces of the black hole. In his final dying moments, Aeson sees a premonition of the future, a pair of blue eyes of a stranger—who later turns out to be Gwen Lark, his fated mate.

Aeson *dies*, and yet his mangled body is saved from compete destruction by the alien *pegasei*, who also bring him back to life.

Aeson becomes a national hero and is awarded the black armband of Honor by his own father. But the experience of dying and resurrection has changed him, and he is back on track with his life goals.

Joining the SPC, he soon advances in his Fleet officer career, becoming *astra daimon*, and a Command Pilot, then the Commander of the SPC.

As a young Kassiopei male, at the age of sixteen Atlantean years (equivalent to twenty and a half Earth years), he is forced by Imperial tradition to participate in the ancient and secret Rite of Sacrifice during which he experiences his first sexual acts, and fathers multiple children (whom he is never permitted to meet) with anonymous women.

Sent on the Earth Mission, Aeson is the Command Pilot of Imperial Command Ship 2 (ICS-2) and second in command of the Atlantean Fleet, under the leadership of IF Commander Manakteon Resoi. (Their command structure is reversed in the SPC, where Aeson is the Commander, and Resoi is the Command Pilot of battle barge War-1.)

Once on Earth, Aeson chooses RQC-3 as his command headquarters, and there is strong indication that he is influenced by seeing Gwen there and subconsciously recognizing her as his destiny.

When the shuttle incident happens and he initially thinks that Gwen was involved in the sabotage (when in fact she rescued him from his burning shuttle after singing it down to safety), Aeson is furious and heartbroken on a profound level he himself doesn't understand.

Once Gwen demonstrates her Logos voice, he takes responsibility of her as an asset "on behalf of Atlantis" and from there on their relationship becomes complex and intertwined.

Aeson begins teaching Gwen advanced voice commands, to ensure her passing Qualification, and assists her as much as possible without showing favoritism on his part. At the end of the Semi-Finals, he pulls her inside the shuttle, burning his own hand.

When Gwen pleads with him on behalf of her Disqualified sister Gracie, Aeson relents and reinstates Gracie, under the reasoning of paying back a debt owed, "a life for a life," since he now knows that Gwen saved his life in the shuttle incident.

Their secret voice training continues, and various complicated feelings and attraction start to develop between the two of them, even though neither Aeson nor Gwen admit it.

After Qualification, Gwen is transferred to Aeson's ark-ship ICS-2 and his direct command. Aeson appoints her as one of his Imperial Aides and refuses to allow her "nonsense" about entering the Games of the Atlantis Grail and becoming a Citizen. Instead, Gwen spends the entirety of the journey taking classes for both career tracks (Cadet and Civilian), and is in daily contact with Aeson during her work duties at the CCO.

During the terrorist hostage situation, Aeson goes in, guns blazing (literally), in order to save Gwen, and shows the extent to which he would go on her behalf.

Their relationship continues to deepen, as Gwen breaks up with her first and only boyfriend Logan Sangre, but Aeson doesn't yet know the reasons for the breakup.

The various Zero-G Dances highlight the stages of their personal involvement, as does the Jump incident when Aeson and Gwen have intense intimate moments while confined in the bunk of his cabin—that's when, for the first time, Aeson loses control over his desire and reveals his burning need for her.

The Red Zero-G Dance only reinforces his loss of control, because Gwen takes it as a challenge to tease and torment him (or simply elicit a reaction), by going on a date with Xelio Vekahat and singing a seductive aria from Carmen. When Aeson mistakenly accuses Gwen of using the *desire voice* on the whole crowd in the Resonance Chamber, he only proves that *he* feels insurmountable desire for *her*. And yet, he is bound by his Imperial duty, and his torment remains internal.

The Yellow Zero-G Dance is the first and only time that Aeson permits himself a weakness, to dance with Gwen, where he almost confesses his love—just as gravity changes. And then, a bombshell revelation comes—Gwen explains why she and Logan broke up—it was over her feelings for Aeson.

This truth, combined with the news that the Imperator plans to take away her freedom and use her as a research subject, gives Aeson the impetus to claim Gwen for himself, at last. It is his true duty to himself.

Nothing and no one must get in the way of this fragile plan. Even Gwen herself must not know his true intentions—hence, his cruel distancing from her when their shuttle lands on Atlantis. It is only at the Imperial Assembly that Aeson reveals his real objective by claiming her as his Bride and Consort before his Imperial Father and all of Atlantis.

In private, after the Assembly, Gwen confronts Aeson with all her pent-up anger and pain, but at last Aeson can be honest with her. He announces his true feelings, and explains to Gwen that he is saving her from a horrible fate at the hands of the Imperator's dark scientists. Aeson tells her that *she matters to him* more than anything and that he is *in love with her*. And in that moment Gwen responds to him by revealing her own deep love, so that they are reconciled.

The blissful happiness of the upcoming Wedding is marred when the Imperator sends Gwen Lark into the Games of the Atlantis Grail under the guise of an Imperial Gift and favor.

This is when Aeson goes to plead for her before his Father (to no avail), and then puts all his efforts into making sure she gets all the training and support imaginable. He gathers experts (including himself) to train Gwen in various martial disciplines, strategy, and other subtleties that are required of a viable Games Contender.

At the start of the Games, Aeson gives Gwen his black armband "on loan" to carry with her during the Games, telling her she must return it to him safely when it's over.

And then he spends every waking moment watching her in the Four Games Stages, and enacting the secret media campaign of the "gold mask," the anonymous terrorist in black called "The Rim." All of it is pre-recorded and meticulously planned in advance, with Anu and Gennio. Every time Gwen is in critical danger, the Rim broadcast interrupts, to distract, and give her a fighting chance.

At the end of the Games, when Gwen raises the Atlantis Grail Monument and reveals the ancient ark-ship, Aeson rushes to her side, and tells her what new dark revelations he learned about his Father, including the fact that the Imperator sent the asteroid to Earth.

The Games are interrupted, and then Gwen learns that her mother has died on Earth. She initially blames Aeson for keeping this secret, but Gracie steps in and takes the responsibility, leaving Gwen and Aeson on good terms.

After Gwen officially becomes a Games Champion, Aeson and Gwen begin dealing with the Wedding preparations. The remaining Lark family members are brought from Earth on a high-speed velo cruiser piloted by Quoni Enutat with a small crew, on Aeson's orders, arriving just in time for the Wedding.

The days leading up to the event, and the day itself, are full of complex and bittersweet joy. Aeson gives Gwen his Love Gift—a key to his Room of Childhood Secrets—which is in fact an ordinary room where Charles Lark and George Lark wait for her.

At the Wedding, Aeson sings a maudlin and heartfelt Earth song by Elvis Presley to Gwen at the Ceremony, gives her an Earth-style wedding ring, and exchanges glorious vows. There are friends and family and much dancing at the Wedding Feast afterwards.

Then comes the Amrevet Night where Aeson and Gwen sing to each other, using the voice of desire, and consummate their physical love at long last. As a Kassiopei male, Aeson is virile, can perform non-stop, and has unusually potent seed requiring a special contraceptive (which the Bride is free to choose to use on this special night).

At the same time, the alien enemy arrives, and Aeson's responsibilities as the Commander of the SPC plunge him into his military duties. Aeson watches helplessly as the various Helios system space stations are destroyed one by one, by the seemingly invincible golden alien spheres.

He mobilizes the Fleet, plans military strategy, while the appearance of the Ghost Moon reveals a cascade of secrets which set in motion the two *astroctadra* missions, and the military action around the system.

When the ancient sarcophagus of Arlenari Kassiopei is discovered, Aeson's perspective and understanding of his own past roots expands. Furthermore, the time comes to reveal to the world that the *pegasei* aliens are sentient beings, and they must be set free.

In the process of the *pegasei* liberation, Aeson and Gwen are given the means to briefly join minds, with the *pegasei* as conduits. The feeling of intimacy is indescribable, and now Aeson knows exactly what Gwen feels and knows, and vice versa. Their soul mate bond deepens to the utmost.

During the final Helios grand alignment *Astroctadra* Mission, Gwen and the others are marooned in space. Aeson drops everything and hurries to save her, alone on a velo-cruiser. At the same time, he is parted with his Father, who goes on a self-sacrificing mission of his own—to conduct the sarcophagus of Arlenari to the Rim of Ae-Leiterra where she and the freed *pegasei* can return to Earth and permanently close the worm hole and the unstable rift on Earth.

In his last moments, Romhutat Kassiopei reconciles with Aeson and Gwen and abdicates his Imperial Throne, going to his death to complete his mission—disappearing in a blaze of light.

Aeson becomes the Archaeon Imperator.

Meanwhile, Gwen saves Earth from the asteroid impact, and uses Starlight to teleport Aeson to her part of space. The ancient alien enemy arrives at last, and Aeson has the chance to confront the ancient "gods" Thoth, Set, Isis, and Horus. He asks them about the true purpose of the Kassiopei bloodline, and is told that they were intended as servant priests, not rulers.

Aeson learns that the Kassiopei genetic material was to be given freely to strengthen and stabilize early ancient homo sapiens. He is also told that the Logos voice is *not* genetic but belongs to everyone—

its potential is within anyone who is capable of intense focus. The Kassiopei Dynasty perpetuated the lie about the uniqueness of the Logos voice in order to retain power and control over the population.

Armed with the knowledge, and still grieving for the loss of his complex father, and the aftermath of the war, Aeson makes love to Gwen (who has forgotten to take her special contraceptive), and the first of their five children is conceived that night.

Romhutat Kassiopei

Role	Archaeon Imperator of Imperial *Atlantida*, Father of Aeson.
Eye Color	Dark Lapis Lazuli Blue
Hair Color	Golden
Height	6'3"
Nickname	Rom
Color Quadrant	Red
Birthdate	Red Ghost Moon 11, 9729 (December 30, 1994)
Zodiac Sign	Fire Delphit (Dolphin)
Home Planet	Atlantis
Physical Appearance	Tall and lean, light bronze skin, coldly handsome, ageless, with chiseled features, dark brows and *wedjat* eyes (natural dark pigment "lined" eyelids), and long golden hair of the Kassiopei Dynasty.
Personality Characteristics	Tyrannical, unpredictable, fiery temper, cynical, contrary, secretive, represses and hides affection, commanding, merciless, burdened by his role, plays the long game.
Strength	Has the Logos voice, skilled at deception, intelligent, wields sarcastic humor, imposing.
Weakness	Sadistic and cruel, has no qualms about hurting loved ones, does not express love, does not understand or recognize it.
Family Members	Father: Etamharat Kassiopei (deceased) Mother: Hesper Kassiopei (deceased) Spouse: Devora Kassiopei née Argosaen Son (1st child): Aeson Kassiopei Daughter (2nd child): Manala Kassiopei
Introduced in	*Qualify* (mentioned by rank only).

Appears in	*Compete, Win, Survive, Aeson: Blue, Aeson: Black.*

Profile and Facts

Romhutat Kassiopei (ROHM-HOO-TAH-T KAH-SEE-OH-PAY) is the Archaeon Imperator of Imperial *Atlantida*, and Aeson's father.

He is a very difficult man, cold but also short-tempered, given to mercurial outbursts and sadistic acts of cruelty. As such, he is a despot toward his family and those who serve him. He frequently uses the *compelling voice* on his son Aeson, daughter Manala, and wife Devora, making them prostrate themselves and bow before him, which they do, even though Aeson cannot be compelled and merely plays along so as not to anger his father.

Romhutat is aligned with the Red Quadrant, so the Imperial Court is Red for the duration of his Imperial reign.

As a member of the Kassiopei Imperial Dynasty, he is a direct descendant of the original Atlantean ruling family on Earth.

Romhutat's parents are both deceased, gone before their time. His mother, Hesper, dies in a tragic accident, so that his father Etamharat, loses the will to live and abdicates his Throne early, in favor of his son, Romhutat.

Soon after, Etamharat goes on a routine Maintenance Mission to the Rim of Ae-Leiterra in order to reinforce the failing Great Quantum Shield, which is normally an Imperial duty, and then sacrifices himself to protect the Fleet, earning the posthumous black armband of Honor. He leaves Romhutat with a secretive and stern message explaining that because the Shield is failing, the ancient alien enemy will soon be able to find them. To avert this, they must return to Earth and close the dimensional rift, and bring the population of Earth back to Atlantis to change the genetic pool.

For Romhutat, this becomes the basis of the Earth Rescue Mission. As the Imperator, he sends an asteroid retrofitted with a resonance chamber and a guidance system to Earth, intending to slam it into the rift—the same way that the ancient aliens tried to close the rift on ancient Atlantis 12,500 Earth years ago.

What follows is the rest of the cascade of events of this story. As soon as the Imperator becomes aware of Gwen Lark and her Logos voice—especially after being informed by his intelligence sources in the Fleet that she Breached during a QS Race and then came back into the Quantum Stream—he takes note of her. And when he realizes that his son Aeson is in love with Gwen, he decides that she must be eliminated in one way or another. In Romhutat's eyes, Gwen is not only a power player but an obstacle to his balance of power and control over his son.

When Romhutat attempts to use his compelling voice on Gwen during her first *eos* bread with the Imperial family, he discovers that she cannot be compelled. This makes her even more intriguing and dangerous.

As soon as Aeson chooses Gwen for his Bride, she becomes officially protected by ancient law, so Romhutat cannot get to her directly. Therefore, he enters her into the Games of the Atlantis Grail, hoping she would be eliminated in the process.

But Gwen survives the Games and even emerges as one of the Champions. And then she completely breaks the Great Quantum Shield when she raises the Atlantis Grail Monument from the ground.

The things Romhutat feared most are now coming to pass. In a fit of anger, he "fries" the orichalcum controls of the asteroid headed for Earth, so that it cannot be stopped in time. It is his small moment of revenge against Gwen standing up to him alongside his son Aeson.

Grudgingly, he must now work together with his son's remarkable Bride to find a solution for the dire events to come. They end up joining Logos voices in a Plural Logos Voice Chorus, but even that is not enough to silence the components of the ancient ark-ship Vimana.

After taking part in the Ghost Moon Mission, the Imperator has to deal with the discovery of Arlenari Kassiopei in her sarcophagus, and The Book of Everything for which he was searching.

And eventually, after the *pegasei* liberation, he has to make the hard decision to give his life in order to manually take the sarcophagus through the wormhole with the *pegasei*.

Romhutat speaks the difficult words to make peace with his son Aeson, daughter Manala, and with Aeson's wife Gwen. He apologizes and admits that he was wrong, and that Aeson did well in choosing Gwen. He also admits that his own wife Devora did a fine job with Manala and that he will always *appreciate* Devora. Finally, he abdicates in favor of his Son, Aeson.

And then, in a flash of light, Romhutat is gone. A truly morally grey character, he is redeemed, at least in part, by his final act.

It is never specified what happens to him, but the dimensional rift on Earth has been successfully sealed.

Aeson quietly grieves for his Father, and after the events of the war, in a special ceremony, awards him a black armband of Honor for finally doing his duty.

Devora Kassiopei

Role	Archaeona Imperatris of Imperial *Atlantida*, Mother of Aeson.
Eye Color	Deep Cobalt Blue
Hair Color	Dark Bronze
Height	5'7"
Color Quadrant	Green
Birthdate	Green Amrevet 6, 9731 (December 27, 1996)
Zodiac Sign	Void Bakriku (Vulture)
Home Planet	Atlantis
Physical Appearance	Agelessly beautiful, reminiscent of Queen Nefertiti, with softly golden skin, dark hair with bronze highlights.
Personality Characteristics	Steadfast and deeply loving, soft-spoken, patient and gentle, long-suffering.
Strength	Fiercely loving, grounded in her faith, full of dignity and compassion.
Weakness	Vulnerable, can be deeply hurt by her husband's cruel outbursts. Locked in a semi-abusive relationship.
Family Members	Father: Tutanamat Argosaen, Lord Mother: Irumala Argosaen, First Lady Spouse: Romhutat Kassiopei Son (1st child): Aeson Kassiopei Daughter (2nd child): Manala Kassiopei
Introduced in	*Compete*
Appears in	*Win, Survive, Aeson: Blue.*

Profile and Facts

Devora Kassiopei (DEH-VOR-ah KAH-SEE-OH-PAY) née Argosaen (AHR-GOH-SAH-EHN) is the Archaeona Imperatris of Imperial *Atlantida* and Aeson's mother.

She is gentle and warm, fiercely protective and loving toward her children and her family, including her difficult spouse Romhutat.

In keeping with her loyal and steadfast personality, Devora is aligned with the Green Quadrant. Her parents, Lord Tutanamat Argosaen and First Lady Irumala Argosaen, are kind and warm-hearted, and the positive and nurturing family dynamic has been passed on to the daughter.

Known as the most beautiful woman of her generation, Devora is chosen as the Imperial Bride and Consort by Romhutat and enters a difficult marriage with a man mostly incapable of love or affection.

Her children, Aeson and Manala are her main source of joy, in addition to her deep faith in the Soul Triumvirate Afterlife Creed.

When Gwen and her siblings arrive on Atlantis, Devora welcomes her future daughter-in-law with all the love and affection she bestows upon her own children. In fact, she does the same to Gracie and Gordie, embracing them warmly and kissing them, while calling them *im saai*.

When George arrives, she accepts him also without question, and immediately notices Charles Lark's grief for his deceased wife. She responds to Charles' grief with a profound understanding, and even berates Romhutat openly for speaking harsh and insensitive things to Charles about Margot.

Devora and Gwen have a heartfelt private talk before the Wedding during which Devora explains some intimate facts about the Kassiopei men and their physical needs, and also tells Gwen about the special Kassiopei contraceptive.

After Romhutat is gone, Devora grieves him, because she does love him, despite everything.

Manala Kassiopei

Role	Imperial Princess of *Atlantida*, Sister of Aeson
Eye Color	Violet-Blue
Hair Color	Golden
Height	5'7"
Nickname	M'nala (bestowed by George)
Color Quadrant	Yellow
Birthdate	Yellow Amrevet 4, 9758 (April 22, 2032)
Zodiac Sign	Magmatic Draguos (Dragon)
Home Planet	Atlantis
Physical Appearance	Delicately beautiful, fragile, slim, with softly golden skin, dark brows and *wedjat* eyes (natural dark pigment "lined" eyelids), and long golden hair of the Kassiopei Dynasty.
Personality Characteristics	Empathetic, sensitive, compassionate, intelligent and inquisitive, sheltered and reclusive, starved for affection, dutiful, intensely focused.
Strength	Has the Logos voice, bluntly honest, sees all creatures as equals, empathetic, loving and optimistic.
Weakness	Sensitive to a fault, vulnerable, has difficulty controlling her emotions, tends to overreact, does not understand sarcasm.
Family Members	Father: Romhutat Kassiopei, Archaeon Imperator of *Atlantida* Mother: Devora Kassiopei, Archaeona Imperatris of *Atlantida* Brother (older): Aeson Kassiopei, Imperial Crown Prince
Introduced in	*Compete*

Appears in	*Win, Survive, Aeson: Blue, Aeson: Black.*

Profile and Facts

Manala Kassiopei (MAH-NAH-lah KAH-SEE-OH-PAY) is the Imperial Princess of Imperial *Atlantida* and Aeson's younger sister.

She is highly sensitive and empathetic, and also emotionally vulnerable because of her strange, sheltered upbringing and isolation, since she grew up surrounded by nannies, tutors, and servants, but no peers. Her Imperial Father pays little attention to her as a person, but at the same time does not permit her to socialize normally with others her age, not even with the young ladies of the Imperial Court. As a result, Manala can be clingy and starved for affection. She admires her brother's *astra daimon* friends, and has a longstanding childhood crush on Xelio.

Curious and creative, Manala is aligned with the Yellow Quadrant. She also has the Logos voice.

As soon as Gwen becomes engaged to Aeson, Manala joyfully latches onto her, and also onto her friends, becoming close with Hasmik Tigranian, Dawn Williams, Laronda Aimes, and the others. She also embraces the Lark family, especially Charles Lark, in whom she finds the father figure she is missing.

She has a large black cat, Khemji, who is her dearest being in the world and her sole companion. When Khemji gets lost, she nearly loses her mind with grief and worry, and throws infantile tantrums until George confronts her somewhat harshly and tells her in no uncertain terms to cut it out.

This shocks Manala so much that, at first, she is furious at George. However, when George goes out of his way to find Khemji and returns him to her (and gets severely scratched up in the process), Manala starts to see George in a different light.

During the Green Zero-G Dance, George is the only one who dares to ask Manala to dance, seeing that she is alone. From this point forward their relationship deepens.

Because of her Logos voice, Manala assists with the *astroctadra* missions. She participates in the first *astroctadra* mission on board

War-5, and is accompanied by Consul Denu, George Lark, and Xelio Vekahat. They are the three people she feels most comfortable around and finds in them a source of strength and succor.

During the final Helios planetary mission, Manala is on board War-6 when the ship is destroyed and she and her companions end up marooned in space.

Manala joins the others in singing together to save Earth.

After the alien war ends, Manala mourns the loss of her Father, but continues to find solace with the Lark family and friends, and her own mother.

Astra Daimon

The following characters are the core group of *astra daimon* who are the closest friends of Aeson. Also included are select acquaintances whose relationship status, interactions, and the important roles they play in the series, are more than casual. There are many others, but they are secondary characters and are described in later sections.

Elikara Vekahat

Role	Aeson's School Friend and First Crush, Fleet Pilot
Eye Color	Brown
Hair Color	Dark Brown
Height	5'8"
Nickname	Eli
Color Quadrant	Yellow
Pilot Call Sign	Aritaak
Birthdate	Red Mar-Yan 13, 9750 (November 25, 2021)
Zodiac Sign	Smoke Sesemet (Horse)
Home Planet	Atlantis
Physical Appearance	Stately and striking, with thick, long dark brown hair, balanced oval face, strong features, aquiline nose, prominent dark brows, dark perceptive eyes. Lithe and proud like the Agnios tree.
Personality Characteristics	Tough and real, playful, sarcastic. Creatively intelligent. Provocative and outgoing, relentless at getting things done and achieving her goals, protective of family and friends.
Strength	Indomitable, driven, fair-minded, true friend.
Weakness	Does not forgive easily.
Family Members	Father: Qeth Vekahat, *Ter* (deceased)

	Mother: Ghara Vekahat née Deksu, Lady Cousin: Xelio Vekahat
Introduced in	*Win*
Appears in	*Win* (mentioned), *Survive* (mentioned), *Aeson Blue, Aeson: Black* (mentioned).

Profile and Facts

Elikara Vekahat (EH-LEE-KAH-rah VEH-kah-HAH-T) is not *astra daimon*, but she is included here because she most likely would have become one, had she lived. She is Aeson's Fleet Cadet School friend and love interest—first crush, and subject of profound admiration.

Elikara is aligned with the Yellow Quadrant. She is a second-year student, one year ahead of Aeson when he enters Fleet Cadet School as a first-year *kefarai*.

Their relationship starts out on the wrong foot, since Elikara is Xelio's cousin, and everyone in the Vekahat Family bears an ancient grudge and hatred toward the Kassiopei Dynasty. The reasons for this are hinted at in *Aeson: Blue*, but never explicitly admitted by the Imperator.

In reality, in ancient times the Vekahat Family was chosen as one of the ten Sacrificed families out of which three are secretly chosen for the actual Rite of Sacrifice. As a result, they had to comply with the tradition of being exiled from the Imperial Court and Poseidon for a generation, regardless of being actually chosen to participate in the Rite of Sacrifice or not. Without consulting the Book of Life (forbidden to all but the Priests of Kassiopei), it remains unknown if the Vekahat are indeed the offspring of the Imperator of that time or mere decoys.

Unfortunately, over the centuries, the Vekahat Family had somehow forgotten the benign reasons for their "banishment" and exile, and started to blame the Imperial Kassiopei for all their misfortunes. This culminates in Xelio's father, Lord Bavaam, committing *im-seki* and leaving young Xelio deprived of his father, forced to become the new Lord, and full of even more hatred toward Kassiopei—and hence, Aeson.

Unlike Xelio, Elikara gives Aeson a chance much sooner. Over the next three years, their relationship evolves into true friendship. There are many pranks played by the students, including the *re-re-xut* bug incident initiated by Elikara, and the time Eli sticks flowers in Aeson's hair. But Aeson is too obtuse to notice when Elikara flirts with him, even though he is enraptured with her.

Only on the eve of Elikara's graduation, do they have a last-minute conversation and reveal some of their mutual feelings. Elikara has just been deployed on her first classified, remote Fleet mission on behalf of the Imperator, and she leaves immediately after the Ceremony, without having a chance to say goodbye.

Over the next year, Aeson does not hear from her. The tragic news comes through Xelio who is notified that Elikara Vekahat and her father Qeth both died in a tragic accident during their mission. When Aeson confronts his Father, the Imperator only admits it was an advance reconnaissance mission to Earth.

Xelio goes nearly mad with grief, and Aeson dyes his hair black while Xel dyes his metallic gold.

Aeson retreats into himself, stalls his career. But even as he dies at Ae-Leiterra, his last vision is not of Elikara's brown eyes, but the blue eyes of another—his future soul mate, Gwen.

Erita Qwas

Role	Aeson's Friend, Green Quadrant Pilot
Eye Color	Pale Hazel
Hair Color	Metallic Gold
Height	5'8"
Nickname	Eri
Color Quadrant	Green
Pilot Call Sign	Tefnut
SPC Pilot Special Affiliation	*Astra Daimon*
Birthdate	Red Amrevet 4, 9751 (December 29, 2022)
Zodiac Sign	Vapor Leontar (Lion)
Home Planet	Atlantis
Physical Appearance	Tall, bulky-muscular, powerful and curvaceous, golden-brown skin, very short gilded hair, sensuous lips, sonorous alto voice.
Personality Characteristics	Warm, fiercely loyal, friendly, no-nonsense, plain-spoken, humorously blunt.
Strength	Ultimate Shield, loyal protector and defender, true friend.
Weakness	Not comfortable with romantic commitment, secretly insecure about her low social status.
Family Members	Mother: Dolati Qwas Father: (out of the picture) Sister (younger): Aeva Qwas
Introduced in	*Qualify*
Appears in	All novels, *Aeson: Blue, Aeson: Black.*

Profile and Facts

Erita Qwas (EH-REE-TAH KWAH-S) is the loyal and indomitable *astra daimon* and heart-sister of Aeson, part of the core group of his closest friends. Erita is the first friend his own age that Aeson makes in Fleet Cadet School, and she is his dormitory bed neighbor.

Erita is a commoner, from a poor family, raised by a single mother, and with one younger sister. Erita's family moves to Poseidon from Bujug, a tiny town in Uotai Province, and she grows up in the Koruut District, near the Golden Bay. She identifies as *amrechira*, the Atlantean equivalent of LGBTQIA+.

Erita is aligned with the Green Quadrant, and graduates near the top of her class, attending Fleet Cadet School on a merit scholarship. She is an exemplary practitioner of her Quadrant's defensive Shield Weapon, and Aeson chooses her to accompany Gwen on their most dangerous final *astroctadra* mission, and protect her with her life— which Erita does, literally.

Erita becomes *astra daimon* before Aeson and is one of the many *daimon* present at his initiation ceremony.

During Qualification, Erita is originally sent to a river settlement in United Industan to scout the best location for Aeson's RQC staff headquarters, until Pennsylvania RQC-3 is permanently chosen.

She is one of the Atlantean Instructors and teaches Combat at RQC-3 and later at the NQC in Colorado.

She is the officer Pilot in charge of Green Quadrant Cadets on ICS-2.

Once on Atlantis, Erita helps Gwen train for the Games of the Atlantis Grail by teaching her advanced Shield and defensive techniques, including the use of *viatoios* armor.

During a Bridal Event at Court, Erita is briefly put down by the obnoxious Lady Tiri (treating her as a servant and demanding she take Gwen's empty plate) because she is not a Citizen or nobility, cruelly reminding Erita that she is a commoner who doesn't belong at the fancy party. Oalla immediately speaks up in her defense, and so does Brie, and ultimately Gwen, who dismisses Lady Tiri. Even so, Erita is made to feel out of place, due to a long-standing sense of insecurity related to her low rank—an insecurity that surfaces during such Imperial Court events.

When the alien war begins, Erita is assigned to accompany and protect Gordie during the first *astroctadra* mission.

During the final Helios mission, Aeson pronounces Erita to be his Shield and entrusts his beloved Gwen to her. When they end up marooned in space, with oxygen running out, Erita gives her life to save Gwen, but is brought back by the *pegasei*. This act of selflessness earns Erita the black armband of Honor, and Aeson's undying gratitude.

When Gwen and Aeson's children are born, they name their youngest child, and third daughter "Erita Hasmik" in honor of Erita Qwas and Hasmik Tigranian.

Keruvat Ruo

Role	Aeson's Friend, Blue Quadrant Pilot
Eye Color	Dark Brown
Hair Color	Metallic Golden
Height	6'7"
Nickname	Ker, Ker-face (by Oalla)
Color Quadrant	Blue
Pilot Call Sign	Sobek
SPC Pilot Special Affiliation	*Astra Daimon*
Birthdate	Yellow Mar-Yan 15, 9751 (July 5, 2023)
Zodiac Sign	Electric Aixi (Swan)
Home Planet	Atlantis
Physical Appearance	Very tall, ebony-black skin, with short tightly curled, gilded hair, extremely handsome, toned and muscular, gorgeously deep voice.
Personality Characteristics	Warm, calm and steady, genuine, easy sense of humor, balanced reactions.
Strength	True friend who has your back, offers unconditional support, does not hesitate to tell the truth, but always with kindness.
Weakness	Can be obtuse when it comes to romantic relationships, somewhat superstitious.
Family Members	Father: Darsuvat Ruo, Lord Mother: Kuz Ruo, First Lady Brother (younger): Valim Ruo Brother (youngest): Ahad Ruo
Introduced in	*Qualify*
Appears in	All novels, *Aeson: Blue, Aeson: Black.*

Profile and Facts

Keruvat Ruo (KEH-RUH-VAH-T ROO-OH) is Aeson's very close friend and *astra daimon* heart-brother, part of the core group of his closest friends.

Ker and Aeson meet while standing in the bathroom line together at their *kefarai* dormitory at Fleet Cadet School, and since then have developed an effortless friendship.

Keruvat is aligned with the Blue Quadrant, and his personality is calm and steady and remarkably well controlled, which makes him an excellent precision marksman and Pilot.

Keruvat is the first of Aeson's circle of friends to be invited into the *astra daimon* brotherhood and sisterhood, after his comet mining mission during which he supervised a pilot team and did high-precision solo flight maneuvers that are now being taught in Fleet Cadet School. He is also one of the many *daimon* present at Aeson's initiation ceremony.

During Qualification on Earth, Ker is originally assigned directly to Pennsylvania RQC-3, along with Oalla Keigeri, to scout the best location for Aeson's RQC staff headquarters, until that same site is permanently chosen.

He is one of the Atlantean Instructors and teaches Combat, usually paired with Oalla Keigeri, at RQC-3 and later at the NQC in Colorado.

After Qualification, upon Aeson's orders, Keruvat personally pilots the shuttle that transfers Gwen from her original ark-ship assignment to ICS-2.

Keruvat is the officer Pilot in charge of Blue Quadrant Cadets on ICS-2.

Once on Atlantis, he joins Aeson and the other *daimon* in training Gwen for the Games of the Atlantis Grail.

Keruvat is Promised to be married to Oalla, and they have been friends and emotionally involved since their earliest Fleet Cadet School days. Keruvat's family is High Court nobility, and Keruvat is formally ninety-eighth generation High Court.

During the first *astroctadra* mission, he is assigned to accompany and assist Anen Qur on War-6.

During the final Helios mission, Aeson pronounces Keruvat to be his Spine without whom "he would not stand up straight," and assigns him to accompany Aeson himself on War-7, to Ishtar.

When Aeson steps down from his post of SPC Commander (due to a conflict of interest, now that he has become Imperator), Keruvat is one of the people he considers for his replacement in that highest position.

Nefir Mekei

Role	Aeson's Acquaintance, Fleet Pilot, ACA Imperial Liaison.
Eye Color	Brown
Hair Color	Metallic Gold
Height	5'11"
Color Quadrant	Yellow
Pilot Call Sign	Anubis
SPC Pilot Special Affiliation	*Astra Daimon*
Birthdate	Green Ghost Moon 8, 9750 (August 21, 2021)
Zodiac Sign	Water Miewu (Cat)
Home Planet	Atlantis
Physical Appearance	Average-height, medium built, short gilded hair, a Deshi-red cast to his skin, balanced features, blunt chin with dimple, prominent brows.
Personality Characteristics	Provocative instructor, values his position as Aeson's "friend," Imperial loyalist, pedantic in his adherence to duty, intelligent and analytical. Socially ingratiating.
Strength	Storyteller power voice, persuasive, intelligent and inquisitive, has much learning to impart. Stubbornly loyal.
Weakness	Divided in his loyalty. His family's Imperial loyalist stance wins out over his friendship with Aeson. Sycophantic.
Family Members	Father: Vaidu Mekei, *Ter* Mother: Lailah Mekei, *Taq* Sister (older): Qroza Mekei Sister (younger): Aibuti Mekei
Introduced in	*Qualify*

| Appears in | All novels, *Aeson: Blue, Aeson: Black.* |

Profile and Facts

Nefir Mekei (NEH-FEER MEH-KEH-ee) is Aeson's peripheral friend and *astra daimon* heart-brother. He attaches himself to the young Imperial Prince from his earliest days in Fleet Cadet School, and is initially considered to be a part of his general circle of friends.

Nefir is aligned with the Yellow Quadrant. He is inquisitive and open-minded, and willing to take chances on people, such as Gwen. He has mastered the *Storyteller* power voice and can be highly persuasive.

Nefir becomes *astra daimon* before Aeson and is one of the many *daimon* present at his initiation ceremony.

The Mekei Family is of lower nobility, and have been fiercely loyal to the Imperial Dynasty for as long as they remember, to the point of being servile and worshipful in their duty, strongly adhering to the Divine cult of Kassiopei. Nefir follows his familial obligations, and although he genuinely cares for Aeson as a person and values their friendship, there is an unbalanced power dynamic. Hence, the nature of this friendship is always strained by his primary allegiance to the Kassiopei Dynasty. In short, his Imperial duties come first.

On the Earth Mission, Nefir is assigned to be a special ACA Imperial Liaison, reporting directly to the Imperator with various intelligence. This ultimately results in the tragic events of Margot Lark's death. During the second phase of the Earth Mission, he is also the ACA Agent in charge of Earth ground operations on board the remaining stealth ark-ship AS-1999 that is secretly orbiting Earth.

During Qualification, Nefir serves as one of the Atlantean Instructors and teaches Atlantis Culture at various sites including RQC-3 and later at the NQC in Colorado. During his classes, Nefir often touches upon provocative subjects—thanks to him, Gwen is made aware of the nature of Atlantean Citizenship and the Games of the Atlantis Grail.

When the rest of the Fleet returns to Atlantis, Nefir remains as ACA Agent in charge of Earth ground operations. His public assignment is to observe the situation on Earth and the asteroid impact. But his real primary objective is to carry out the final clandestine orders—making sure that the manually-guided asteroid strikes the dimensional rift on Earth.

At the same time, Nefir is given by Aeson the responsibility of rescuing the remaining Lark Family from the surface. Unknown to Aeson, his orders are countermanded by the Imperator who orders Nefir to stall the rescue long enough to make sure that Gwen's mother dies, with her terminal cancer left untreated.

Nefir is genuinely torn. He wants to do Aeson's bidding, but he must obey his Imperator. Unfortunately, Imperial duty wins. Nefir calls in endless unsubstantiated promises and excuses from orbit to Charles, Margot, and George, who remain down on Earth's surface.

In the process of his many, tense and awkward, deception-filled video conversations with the Larks, he lets slip that Gwen and Aeson are in love and getting married. It is how Margot finds out about her daughter's happiness—which ends up being the one good thing that Nefir does for Margot.

After Margot passes away, Nefir lets Aeson know, but does not yet inform the Imperator, promising Aeson to hold off until the Games are over. This is his unsuccessful attempt at playing both sides. The small delay helps Gwen to retain her focus in the Games.

Aeson tells Nefir that he is not to contact him again unless it is something directly work-related, and he is not to address him by the nickname "Kass" which is only permitted to his friends. Too late, Nefir realizes how badly he has miscalculated, and how much he has lost. His friendship and personal relationships with Aeson and the other *astra daimon* have been irrevocably damaged.

In the end, Nefir assists Gwen in saving Earth. To give him credit, he does this even before learning that Romhutat Kassiopei has abdicated in favor of his son, and Aeson is now the Imperator and his direct authority.

However, once he does find out, it only reinforces Nefir's stance. His new loyalties are now clear-cut, and there is no more conflict between friendship and duty.

His new Imperator and Imperatris might feel otherwise.

Oalla Keigeri

Role	Aeson's Friend, Yellow Quadrant Pilot
Eye Color	Steely Turquoise Blue
Hair Color	Metallic Golden
Height	5'7½"
Color Quadrant	Yellow
Pilot Call Sign	Bast
SPC Pilot Special Affiliation	*Astra Daimon*
Birthdate	Green Pegasus 11, 9751 (October 10, 2022)
Zodiac Sign	Ice Astroctadra (Four-Point Star)
Home Planet	Atlantis
Physical Appearance	Beautiful and doll-like, chiseled features, beautifully defined curving eyebrows, hourglass figure, combination of curves and muscular strength. Shoulder-length, wavy, gilded hair.
Personality Characteristics	Harmoniously friendly and confident, excellent social skills, outgoing, subtle but tough.
Strength	A great friend, brings out the best in others, perceptive and full of personal insight. Confident and commanding.
Weakness	Can be pushy and demanding. Comes across as a hard and overbearing taskmaster.
Family Members	Father: Desher Keigeri, Lord (goes by *Ter* in media relations) Mother: Xilith Keigeri, First Lady (deceased) Aunt (maternal): Emelea Ynaet Brother (older): Madur Keigeri Brother (younger): Raeth Keigeri Brother (youngest): Ulum Keigeri

Introduced in	*Qualify*
Appears in	All novels, *Aeson: Blue, Aeson: Black.*

Profile and Facts

Oalla Keigeri (OH-AHL-lah KAY-GEH-ree) is Aeson's very close friend and *astra daimon* heart-sister, part of the core group of his closest friends.

She meets Aeson in the first few days of Fleet Cadet School. After Aeson gets into a fight with Xelio over a dormitory cot, she picks up after him and straightens his bed, because she finds this behavior intolerable and the messed-up bed an embarrassment for the Imperial Kassiopei.

Later, Oalla serves as the social glue to bring everyone in their core friendship group together.

She is aligned with the Yellow Quadrant, and is imaginative, clever and curious. Quick on her feet and with her hands, Oalla wields the Nets and Cords Yellow Quadrant Weapons with great skill.

In Fleet Cadet School, Oalla is quickly attracted to Keruvat with his calm poise, gentle strength, and "no drama" approach. She also defeats him during their Combat Demo in class and Ker is duly impressed. Their mutual attraction and bond grows all through their school years and deepens, until they are an inseparable couple, Promised to each other in marriage.

Oalla becomes *astra daimon* before Aeson. She is the person who tricks and lures Aeson into coming to the initiation site under traditional false pretenses, and is one of the many *daimon* present at his initiation ceremony.

During Qualification on Earth, Oalla is originally assigned directly to Pennsylvania RQC-3, along with Keruvat Ruo, to scout the best location for Aeson's RQC staff headquarters, until that same site is permanently chosen.

She is one of the Atlantean Instructors and teaches both Agility and Combat, usually paired with Keruvat Ruo, and occasionally with Erita Qwas, at RQC-3 and later at the NQC in Colorado.

Oalla sees potential in Gwen early on, despite her awkwardness during training at the Pennsylvania RQC-3. She is the first of Aeson's friends to notice Aeson's interest in Gwen, and reveals to Gwen who he really is and that "she matters to him," just before the Qualification Finals.

Oalla is the officer Pilot in charge of Yellow Quadrant Cadets on ICS-2.

Oalla helps Aeson come to terms with his feelings for Gwen after the Red Zero-G Dance.

Once on Atlantis, Oalla helps Gwen train for the Games of the Atlantis Grail by teaching her advanced Nets and Cords and defensive techniques, including the use of a special razor-sharp *viatoios* net that can be used to wrap oneself against an attacker, and then flung to wrap the same enemy. This technique saves Gwen's life and allows her to overpower Thalassa during the Games.

During a Bridal Event at Court, Oalla stands up for her heart-sister Erita when Lady Tiri demeans her. Oalla also reveals that she is two-hundred-ninety-third generation, High Court nobility, and her family comes from the Eastern Duinaat Province.

During the first *astroctadra* mission, Oalla is assigned to accompany and assist Gwen on the moon Mar-Yan.

During the final Helios mission, Aeson calls Oalla his Guiding Star and puts her in charge of Gordie Lark on War-8, under the command of Lafaoh Ungreb of Bastet, together with Charles Lark with the urn of Margot Lark, their destination being Tammuz.

When Aeson steps down from his post of SPC Commander (due to a conflict of interest, now that he has become Imperator), Oalla is one of the people he considers for his replacement in that highest position.

Aeson and Gwen name their second daughter, "Oalla Ann" in honor of both their friends.

Quoni Enutat

Role	Aeson's Friend, Fleet Pilot
Eye Color	Dark Brown
Hair Color	Black, gilded at the tips.
Height	5'9"
Color Quadrant	Blue
Pilot Call Sign	Ixion
SPC Pilot Special Affiliation	*Astra Daimon*
Birthdate	Red Pegasus 19, 9750 (November 2, 2021)
Zodiac Sign	Air Sebeku (Crocodile)
Home Planet	Atlantis
Physical Appearance	Average height, medium build. Lean, elegant features, reminiscent of Earth Asian, chiseled, aristocratic jawline, golden-bronze skin, short black spiked hair gilded only at the tips, deep voice.
Personality Characteristics	Crisp and businesslike, dignified and reserved, serious and controlled, calm but can also be daredevil. Highly observant, brisk mannered, rarely smiles.
Strength	Very organized, precise, and efficient. Detail oriented and observant. Courageous.
Weakness	Risk-taking tendencies.
Family Members	Father: Ladmar Enutat, *Ter* (deceased) Mother: Chirima Enutat, *Taq* (deceased) Uncle: Ungiz Enutat Brother (older): Asdai Enutat
Introduced in	*Win*
Appears in	*Win* (mentioned), *Survive, Aeson: Black.*

Profile and Facts

Quoni Enutat (KOO-OH-NEE EH-NUH-TAHT) is Aeson's friend and *astra daimon* heart-brother.

He is aligned with the Blue Quadrant, although during his placement test and early decision process he admittedly took his time deciding between Blue and Red.

Quoni becomes *astra daimon* before Aeson and is one of the many *daimon* present at his initiation ceremony.

During the Earth Mission, Quoni is assigned to AS-1999, where he has a lower rank and clearance than Nefir, but notices that Nefir is stalling the rescue of the Larks. He observes a pattern over several days then informs Aeson.

After Margot dies, Nefir is confronted, and Charles and George are rescued and brought on board the ark-ship, Quoni is ordered by Aeson to bring the Lark Family and their possessions immediately to Atlantis via a high velocity cruiser. Quoni is to exceed the maximum rated speed in the Quantum Stream, in order to arrive as soon as possible.

Quoni carries out these orders perfectly, arriving with the Larks before the Wedding. He takes excellent care of Charles and George while they are on board the velo-cruiser, and delivers them safely and discreetly to the Imperial Palace.

During the alien war, Quoni figures out a stalling technique to slow down the alien golden grid from forming at Tammuz. Thanks to his excellent instincts and piloting skills, the Fleet gains some advantage over the enemy.

After many of the Helios system *astroctadra* mission participants are marooned in space, Quoni is sent to rescue Manala and her contingent. However, because Gwen uses Starlight to rescue everyone, Quoni and the rest of the rescue parties end up sweeping the deep space coordinates of the battle barge debris for other survivors instead.

Tiliar Vahad

Role	Aeson's Friend, Fleet Pilot (deceased)
Eye Color	Brown
Hair Color	Black with Metallic Gold on top
Height	5'6"
Color Quadrant	Blue
Pilot Call Sign	Khonsu
SPC Pilot Special Affiliation	*Astra Daimon*
Birthdate	Blue Ghost Moon 3, 9750 (August 3, 2022)
Zodiac Sign	Starlight Akhet (Horizon)
Home Planet	Atlantis
Physical Appearance	Shorter than average, introspective and calm eyes, flat nose, bronze skin, features reminiscent of Earth Asian.
Personality Characteristics	Kind and mild-mannered, soft-spoken, reserved, capable of gentle humor, hardworking, precise, extremely honest.
Strength	Empathetic, affectionate, and dependable friend. Dreams big, of flying to the stars.
Weakness	Tends to not assert himself.
Family Members	Father: Rhanat Vahad (deceased) Mother: Ilinai Vahad Sister (older): Mara Vahad Brother (younger): Faimut Vahad Brother (youngest): Jodar Vahad
Introduced in	*Qualify*
Appears in	*Qualify* (mentioned), *Aeson: Blue, Aeson: Black.*

Profile and Facts

Tiliar Vahad (TEE-LEE-AHR VAH-HAH-D) is Aeson's friend and *astra daimon* heart-brother, part of the core group of his closest friends.

Tiliar is the second friend his own age that Aeson makes in Fleet Cadet School, and he is his dormitory bed neighbor.

He is a commoner, from a poor working family, from Defo, a small quarry town in the Southeast Raia Province. His family has worked in the quarries, doing manual mining labor and also working with tech, for more than two generations. His father dies in a mine collapse, and his mother is barely able to make ends meet, along with Tiliar, his older sister Mara, and two younger brothers Faimut and Jodar.

Tiliar works his way through Fleet Cadet School, returning to work the quarries in his home town between school breaks to single-handedly earn the funds to cover his tuition, since his family is unable to pay at all. He is a year older than others in his class because he did not have enough saved up to cover his tuition until a little later.

Tiliar is aligned with the Blue Quadrant. He becomes *astra daimon* before Aeson and is one of the many *daimon* present at his initiation ceremony.

In Fleet Cadet School, at their first Zero-G Dance, Tiliar dances with Chimaida, a girl he asked to be his date. He also takes part in the various school pranks, and is there for the *re-re-xut* bug incident.

On the Earth Mission, early during Qualification, Tiliar Vahad is one of the three Pilots killed in the first shuttle that explodes in the air, during the shuttle sabotage incident at RQC-3. At the time of his death, he has attained the position of Pilot First Rank, is nineteen years old, and has served seven years in the Fleet.

Tiliar likes the taste of Earth raspberries.

Tiliar's tragic death (and the death of the other two, Chiar Nuridat and Felekamen Gori) sends Aeson and the other Atlanteans into profound grief, disrupts Qualification, and sets the course of many pivotal events, including Gwen discovering her Logos voice and working with Aeson.

Xelio Vekahat

Role	Aeson's Friend, Red Quadrant Pilot
Eye Color	Dark Brown
Hair Color	Raven Black, undyed.
Height	6'4"
Nickname	Xel
Color Quadrant	Red
Pilot Call Sign	Shamash
SPC Pilot Special Affiliation	*Astra Daimon*
Birthdate	Blue Pegasus 23, 9751 (October 10, 2023)
Zodiac Sign	Gravity Uraeus (Serpent)
Home Planet	Atlantis
Physical Appearance	Tall, with a stone-cold handsome face of lean angles. Well defined brows, aquiline nose, dark brown eyes. Very dark, "black-hole" black hair, long and straight, undyed. Deep bronze skin, perfectly sculpted, muscular body, low and cool voice.
Personality Characteristics	Intense, secretly emotional, with icy outward demeanor that can erupt in rage or sarcasm if provoked. Can be terribly charming and persuasive, suave and confident, with a magnetic smile. Driven and relentless.
Strength	Loyal and fiercely loving. Sensual and seductive. Goes after what he wants and never gives up. Likes a challenge. Top swordsman.
Weakness	Angry and volatile. Overly competitive. Long memory, carries a grudge.
Family Members	Father: Bavaam Vekahat, Lord (deceased) Mother: Aduar Vekahat, First Lady

	Cousin: Elikara Vekahat (deceased)
Introduced in	*Qualify*
Appears in	All novels, *Aeson: Blue, Aeson: Black.*

Profile and Facts

Xelio Vekahat (K-SEH-lee-oh Veh-kah-HAH-T) or (ZEH-lee-oh) is Aeson's very close friend and *astra daimon* heart-brother, part of the core group of his closest friends. He is also his lifelong friendly rival—their rivalry started out in a complicated love-hate relationship.

Xelio is the first boy that Aeson notices on his first day at Fleet Cadet School, because of his undyed black hair, and they immediately get into a physical fight. Xelio is also the cousin of Elikara, the fascinating girl who has caught Aeson's interest.

Xelio is the one who gives Aeson his nickname "Kass"—originally as a slur and putdown, but Aeson likes it and adopts it with his friends.

Xelio, along with everyone in the noble but impoverished House Vekahat (based in the Southern Uru Province), bears an ancient grudge and hatred toward the Kassiopei Dynasty. The reasons for this are hinted at in *Aeson: Blue*, but never explicitly admitted by the Imperator.

In reality, in ancient times the Vekahat Family was chosen as one of the ten Sacrificed families out of which three are secretly chosen for the actual Rite of Sacrifice. As a result, they had to comply with the tradition of being exiled from the Imperial Court and Poseidon for a generation, regardless of being actually chosen to participate in the Rite of Sacrifice or not. Without consulting the Book of Life (forbidden to all but the Priests of Kassiopei), it remains unknown if the Vekahat are indeed the offspring of the Imperator of that time or mere decoys.

Unfortunately, over the centuries, the Vekahat Family had somehow forgotten the benign reasons for their "banishment" and exile, and started to blame the Imperial Kassiopei for all their misfortunes. This culminates in Xelio's father, Lord Bavaam, committing *im-seki* and leaving young Xelio deprived of his father, forced to become the new Lord (one hundred and tenth generation, High Court), and full of even more hatred toward Kassiopei—and hence, Aeson.

After several angry confrontations, including sparring in Combat class, young Xelio and Aeson have a profound and honest conversation, and come to an understanding that eventually grows into deep affection and friendship.

News of Elikara's death brings them both even closer together. For the first and only time in their lives, Aeson dyes his hair black to show his mourning for Eli and his sympathy to Vekahat, while Xelio dyes his hair gold to show his allegiance to this *one* particular Kassiopei.

Xelio is aligned with the Red Quadrant, bold and aggressive, and is the top-rated swordsman in his graduating class at Fleet Cadet School, besting Aeson.

Xel becomes *astra daimon* before Aeson. He is in fact the one who "calls him out" at his initiation ceremony. This means that he is the person who nominated and recommended Aeson for the honor in the first place. The *astra daimon* tradition ritual includes an initial nomination by one of the members, which is later repeated to the candidate in the form of *"You have been called out by one of your peers and you must answer."*

During Qualification, Xel is originally sent to a village in southern China to scout the best location for Aeson's RQC staff headquarters, until Pennsylvania RQC-3 is permanently chosen.

He is one of the Atlantean Instructors and teaches Combat at RQC-3 and later at the NQC in Colorado.

Xelio is the Instructor partially responsible for Gwen earning the nickname "Shoelace Girl." During Combat class, she ends up last, without a practice weapon, and makes her own "weapon" on the spot by pulling out her shoelaces and tying them together to form a cord (Nets and Cords are the Yellow Quadrant weapons). This impresses him so much that later he uses this to convince Aeson not to

Disqualify her and Hasmik during the Quadrant punishment session at the Arena Commons.

Xelio first notices Hasmik Tigranian during that session, and is not only impressed but deeply touched by her stoic, quiet demeanor and act of endurance. Hasmik stands on her injured foot, and ends up fainting from the pain, despite Gwen's brave attempt to help her.

From there on, Hasmik gets on Xelio's radar, and he continues to closely observe her caring interactions with Gwen and the others.

Indeed, after several attempts (much later) to ask Hasmik to dance with him, her repeated refusals only serve to intrigue him further. Hasmik is the one woman who represents his secret ideal. Neither flashy nor strikingly beautiful, she is the opposite of flirtatious. But just like her friend Gwen, Hasmik is strong, quietly courageous, and *real*, in her own, warm, and genuine way.

Xelio is the officer Pilot in charge of Red Quadrant Cadets on ICS-2.

He helps Gwen train at the gym during the journey from Earth to Atlantis. In his usual habit of trying to get a rise out of Aeson, he invites Gwen to go as his official Date to the Red Zero-G Dance, and discovers she is more than he bargained for—a spectacular queen, fit for the Imperial Court, and a true match for Aeson.

Once on Atlantis, Xelio continues to help Gwen train for the Games of the Atlantis Grail, this time by teaching her to run first instead of fight. During this training, he is ruthless and "hands-on" in order to emphasize the deadly ordeal ahead of her. This briefly invokes Aeson's jealous anger.

Xelio is tactfully aware that Aeson's sister Manala has a young crush on him, but he never encourages her, and maintains the strict distance because of her rank. He does not ask Manala to dance during the Imperial Wedding which makes her very upset. As a result, she runs away, and then leaves a window open in her bedroom, allowing her cat Khemji to escape. Later on, Aeson asks Xelio to talk to Manala (she refuses to eat because of missing Khemji), and during their interaction, Xelio acts the gentleman, while Manala comes to understand that theirs is only a good friendship and nothing more.

As one of the people Manala trusts the most, Xelio is assigned to protect her on War-5 during the first *astroctadra* mission.

During the final Helios system mission, Aeson pronounces Xelio to be his Sword, and assigns him to accompany Manala again, this time on War-6. When the battle barge War-6 is destroyed, Xelio, Manala, Hasmik, George, and many others end up marooned in space.

This is when Xelio's feelings for Hasmik fully emerge. She single-handedly and bravely saves everyone in their *depet*, and then dies (before being brought back by the *pegasei* aliens), and Xelio reveals his desperation and grief. Then, once Hasmik is safe and hospitalized (and shares the room with Erita), Xelio and Hasmik finally give in to their mutual feelings for each other (and drive Erita crazy with their displays of sentiment).

When Aeson steps down from his post of SPC Commander (due to a conflict of interest, now that he has become Imperator), Xelio is one of the people he considers for his replacement in that highest position.

Friends and Allies

The following characters are the core group of Earth friends, associates, and peers who are the closest friends of Gwen. Also included are select acquaintances whose relationship status, interactions, and the important roles they play in the series are more than casual.

Blayne Dubois

Role	Gwen's Friend
Eye Color	Blue
Hair Color	Brown
Height	5'10"
Nickname	Bee One (by Gracie)
Color Quadrant	Yellow
Qualification Semi-Finals Dorm	Yellow Quadrant Dorm Eight
Qualification Finals	Team USA 14D
RQC-3 Rank (out of 6,023)	#1,692
Birthdate	November 26, 2032 (Blue Ghost Moon 15, 9758)
Zodiac Sign	Sagittarius
Home Planet	Earth
Physical Appearance	Longish, brown wispy hair falling over his blue eyes, light skin, muscular arms, thin lower body.
Personality Characteristics	Smart loner, introspective, calm, fatalistic, dry sense of humor. Aspires to do something with his life. Often escapes inside his head by reading. Tenacious and brave.
Strength	Does not let circumstances stop him, a fighter. Skillful on the hoverboard, masters the Limited Mobility (LM) Forms.

Weakness	Negative thinking and self-esteem issues, chronically blames himself.
Family Members	Father: Mark Dubois Mother: Emily Dubois Sister (older): Laurie Dubois Brother (younger): Jake Dubois
Introduced in	*Qualify*
Appears in	All novels, *Aeson: Black.*

Profile and Facts

Blayne Dubois is Gwen's friend whom she meets during Qualification at the RQC-3. However, she first notices him earlier during the Pre-Qualification hoverboard test at Mapleroad Jackson High School.

He is the "wheelchair kid" who inspires the Four Gees and the rest of the students when he tenaciously attempts to use the hoverboard at the Pre-Qualification site. Without the use of his legs, he lifts himself with his hands, lies down flat on top of the board and holds on, persevering long enough to pass the test.

Blayne feels profound guilt that he managed to pass Preliminary Qualification while his sister Laurie (who wants to be a doctor) and brother Jake (widely talented, going to change the world) did not.

Blayne is aligned with the Yellow Quadrant and assigned to Yellow Quadrant Dorm Eight at the Pennsylvania RQC-3.

Gwen makes friends with Blayne despite himself, by being pushy and frankly tactless, awkwardly "saving" him from the dorm bullies even when he tells her he doesn't need her help. Eventually Blayne comes to accept that Gwen is just ridiculous but means well, and he tolerates her—until they really are friends.

When Gwen goes to Aeson's office after her punishment, she is tasked by Aeson to assist while Aeson trains Blayne in the special "wounded or otherwise incapacitated soldier" Atlantean Combat style called Limited Mobility Forms (LM). They are also taught the Grip of Friendship. Through this regular evening training (while she also receives her voice training from Aeson, after Blayne leaves), Gwen gets to know and understand Blayne even better.

Going into the Semi-Finals, Blayne ranks #1,692 at RQC-3, and picks Denver for his competition arena, where he immediately commandeers a hoverboard and uses LM forms to survive.

Blayne earns an unspecified number of Final Points at the NQC, and is assigned to Team USA 14D in the Finals.

During the last moments of the final sprint, flying through the volcanic tube toward the surface, Blayne uses the Grip of Friendship to save Gracie who has lost control of her hoverboard. In that moment, Gracie "imprints" on him, and starts to pay attention to him.

Blayne Qualifies and is assigned to an unspecified ark-ship, then transferred by Aeson's orders to ICS-2. He chooses Fleet Cadet as his life choice, and is assigned to the Yellow Quadrant, Navigation and Guidance, Cadet Deck Four Barracks.

Blayne is given his own hoverboard permanently. In addition to his regular Cadet duties, he teaches Limited Mobility (LM) Forms to Cadets all around the Fleet, on different ark-ships.

During the Blue Zero-G Dance, Blayne and Gracie spend time together and end up dancing in zero gravity, which marks the beginning of their relationship. Blayne calls Gracie "Lark Two."

Blayne ranks at #351 at the beginning of the first Cadet Quantum Stream Race and earns an 83% Fleet Score at the end.

He ranks at #173 at the beginning of the second QS Race (with Pilot Partner Leon Madongo), then earns a 93% Fleet Score, and ranks at #18 for his ark-ship at the end.

On Atlantis, Blayne supports Gwen throughout her Games training, and together with Dawn contacts Arbiter Tamira Bedut to help with her legal affairs.

At the Imperial Wedding, Blayne wears a special orichalcum hover-vest obtained for him by Hasmik. He also connects with Gracie's father Charles Lark over books and other shared subjects.

He is one of the six *shìrén* Cadet Pilots assigned to Gwen's final PRT unit on the *Pegasei* Retrieval Khenneb Mission.

During the alien war, Blayne is deployed with the other Earth Cadets, and serves on War-1, to defend Atlantis.

Chiyoko Sato

Role	Gwen's Friend and Second Pilot Partner
Eye Color	Dark Brown
Hair Color	Raven black with red highlights
Height	5'7½"
Color Quadrant	Green
Birthdate	September 6, 2030 (Green Ghost Moon 23, 9757)
Zodiac Sign	Virgo
Home Planet	Earth
Physical Appearance	Big, tall, and husky, with round face and permanently stressed expression. Tries to make herself disappear, slouches. Deep, soft voice.
Personality Characteristics	Highly intelligent, non-confrontational. Verbally proficient. Quiet and thoughtful.
Strength	Cooperative, supportive, excellent partner.
Weakness	Shy, self-effacing. Extremely nervous and tends to panic and hyperventilate when stressed.
Family Members	Father: Koichi Sato Mother: Maki Sato
Introduced in	*Compete*
Appears in	*Compete, Win, Survive.*

Profile and Facts

Chiyoko Sato is Gwen's friend and second Cadet Pilot Partner (after Gwen is unpaired from Hugo Moreno). She first appears in *Compete*. Gwen notices her in Pilot Training Class, then talks with her in Language Class, where Chiyoko shows her intelligence and erudition and gives an exemplary answer to the Language Instructor about similes and metaphors.

Chiyoko has chosen Fleet Cadet as her life choice and is assigned to the Green Quadrant, Brake and Shields, Cadet Deck Three Barracks on ICS-2.

During the Blue Zero-G Dance, Chiyoko is a solitary wallflower, and Aeson graciously asks her to dance—which sets in motion the breakup between Gwen and Logan.

When the Cadets are permitted to change their Pilot Partners, Gwen asks Chiyoko to be her new Pilot Partner, and neither one of them is pushy or controlling, so their Pilot and Co-Pilot turns are evenly balanced. In addition, Gwen suggests they split up the Roles of Red and Green (Thrust and Brake) and Yellow and Blue (Navigation and Adjustment) to accommodate their personal talents. Thus, Gwen handles Thrust and Navigation, while Chiyoko does Brake and Adjustment, and their flight performance drastically improves.

Chiyoko (paired with Gwen) ranks at #314 at the beginning of the second Cadet Quantum Stream Race. She earns a 96% Fleet Score and ranks at #5 for her ark-ship at the end of the second QS Race.

Once on Atlantis, Chiyoko gets assigned to the Poseidon Fleet Headquarters technical division.

She supports Gwen throughout the Games and after, during the Bridal Events. At the Imperial Wedding, Chiyoko dances with Aeson's Imperial Aide Gennio Rukkat.

She also socializes with Gennio at the Green Zero-G Dance.

During the alien war, Chiyoko is deployed with the other Earth Cadets, and serves on War-1, to defend Atlantis.

Dawn Williams

Role	Gwen's Friend
Eye Color	Brown
Hair Color	Black
Height	5'5½"
Color Quadrant	Yellow
Qualification Semi-Finals Dorm	Yellow Quadrant Dorm Eight
Qualification Finals	Team USA 14A
RQC-3 Rank (out of 6,023)	#98
Birthdate	December 30, 2032 (Green Amrevet 20, 9759)
Zodiac Sign	Capricorn
Home Planet	Earth
Physical Appearance	Slim, medium height, young-looking, with waist-long black hair, dark eyes, light brown skin.
Personality Characteristics	Quiet and reserved, dignified, loyal, unassuming, no-nonsense. Prefers simplicity and no drama. Never brags.
Strength	Principled and strong, high achiever.
Weakness	Does not always sufficiently communicate what she feels or needs.
Family Members	Father: Samuel Greene (deceased) Mother: Valerie Williams
Introduced in	*Qualify*
Appears in	All novels

Profile and Facts

Dawn Williams is Gwen's friend, introduced to her by Laronda, during Qualification.

Dawn is a fourteen-year-old Native member of the Oneida Nation, from Oneida, New York. She has lost her father to cancer, early in life, and lives with her mother. She identifies as LGBTQIA+.

Dawn is assigned to Yellow Quadrant Dorm Eight, and quietly excels during Qualification training.

When Laronda is falsely accused of sabotage in the shuttle incident, Dawn goes with Gwen to plead on her behalf, and Gwen ends up being accused in Laronda's place, while Laronda is acquitted and released from jail.

Going into the Semi-Finals, Dawn ranks #98 at RQC-3, and picks New York for her competition arena.

Dawn earns 201 Final Points at the NQC, Section Fourteen, and is assigned to Team USA 14A in the Finals.

She Qualifies and ends up on Ark-Ship 809, together with Hasmik and Laronda (both of whom she saves during the last moments of the Finals). Having no interest in fighting, Dawn wants to settle down in peace, study biology and agriculture and raise the Atlantean equivalent of chickens. She chooses Civilian as her life choice and is assigned to Yellow Quadrant, Residential Deck Four Dormitory.

Once on Atlantis, Dawn obtains a job in the bio-analysis division of the Earth Seed Bank of Heri Agriculture, at the Poseidon Headquarters.

She supports Gwen in her preparation for the Games. Together with Blayne, Dawn contacts the high-powered Poseidon arbiter Tamira Bedut, who is Erita's ex-girlfriend, in order to handle Gwen's citizenship and immigration legal affairs.

Dawn accompanies Gwen to various Bridal events.

At the Imperial Wedding, Dawn dances casually with George and then with Xelio to prove a humorous point. Then Dawn and Tamira dance together, hinting at the beginning of an intimate relationship.

Gabriella "Brie" Walton

Role	Gwen's Ally, Member of Team Lark (Games of the Atlantis Grail)
Eye Color	Brown
Hair Color	Dark Brown with Purple highlights
Height	5'6"
Nickname	Brie
Color Quadrant	Red
Birthdate	October 4, 2028 (Yellow Ghost Moon 26, 9755)
Zodiac Sign	Libra
Home Planet	Earth
Physical Appearance	Medium height, toned body, waist-long, straight dark hair with purple streak highlights.
Personality Characteristics	Aggressively sarcastic, rebellious. Cool and calculating, dry sense of humor. Cynical and disillusioned. Great acting skills. Capable of deep loyalty. Fights for a cause. Master manipulator.
Strength	Mastermind and brilliant strategist. Loyal and protective, fierce fighter. Highly intelligent.
Weakness	Overly cynical, mistrusts everyone, assumes ulterior motives. Afraid of confined spaces (claustrophobic).
Family Members	Father: Michael Walton (deceased) Mother: Ophelia Walton (deceased) Grandfather: Peter Walton, Admiral
Introduced in	*Compete*
Appears in	*Compete, Win, Survive.*

Profile and Facts

Gabriella "Brie" Walton is Gwen's ally in the Games and member of
Team Lark, who eventually becomes a friend.

Originally from Iowa (and a possible military upbringing), Brie
is first introduced in *Compete* as the girl with purple streaked hair,
and the girlfriend of alpha bully and Terra Patria terrorist Trey Smith.
In reality she is a member of Earth Union—a high-level operative
who pretends to be Trey's girlfriend and has infiltrated the terrorist
organization in order to agitate on behalf of Earth Union.

Brie is assigned to the Red Quadrant, Drive and Propulsion,
Cadet Deck One Barracks on board ICS-2.

Brie masterminds the multi-ship terrorist attempt to take over the
Atlantean Fleet that results in the hostage situation in which Gwen
and Blayne nearly die and Aeson has to come in, guns blazing, to save
them.

After the terrorist uprising is put down, Brie is captured and
incarcerated for involvement with the hostage incident and more. She
is interrogated by Logan Sangre, a fellow Earth Union operative (with
a lesser clearance level) who reassessed the moral and ethical
implications of the EU and Earth government directives, switched
sides and warned Aeson about the uprising.

Once on Atlantis, Brie continues to be incarcerated at the
Poseidon Central Correctional Facility (PCCF), with Logan in charge
of her, until she sees Gwen on the media feeds and decides to use this
opportunity to make a deal—as a third option (instead of execution or
life imprisonment), she will enter the Games of the Atlantis Grail
along with Gwen to protect her, in exchange for disclosing valuable
intelligence—everything she knows about Earth Union and the
current plans of Earth governments.

Aeson accepts the deal, and Logan enters Brie into the Games in
the Entrepreneur Category.

Brie immediately saves Gwen from poisoning by killing
treacherous Larahat Sei, and becomes a valuable member of Team

Lark, continuing to protect Gwen though all the Four Stages to the best of her abilities.

At the end of the Games, Brie wins in her Category and is Top Ten Champion #7, with 3,821 AG Points.

Brie's Champion Wishes include a release from Correctional and decent living arrangements, having Logan Sangre be at her beck and call for three months (in revenge for interrogating her), and reinstatement as an Earth Cadet in the Imperial Fleet.

During Kokayi's Parade, Brie tells Gwen about her amusing and sadistic arrangement with Logan and how she is getting back at him.

At the Imperial Wedding, Brie and Logan dance together, and then again are seen together at the Green Zero-G Dance. It appears that there is something more between them now, a complicated relationship.

Brie is one of the six *shìrén* Pilots assigned to Gwen's final PRT mission.

After the alien war is over, Brie plans to return to Earth, and Logan decides to follow her.

Gwen gives Logan's special gift, the knife that he once gave her, to Brie, since she is now his special someone.

Hasmik Tigranian

Role	Gwen's Friend
Eye Color	Brown
Hair Color	Dark Brown
Height	5'4"
Color Quadrant	Yellow
Qualification Semi-Finals Dorm	Yellow Quadrant Dorm Eight
Qualification Finals	Team USA 14D
RQC-3 Rank (out of 6,023)	#5,023
Birthdate	February 27, 2030 (Blue Pegasus 8, 9756)
Zodiac Sign	Pisces
Home Planet	Earth
Physical Appearance	Small, thin and petite, with dark brown wavy hair, brown eyes, a pleasant, kind face, and a gentle smile.
Personality Characteristics	Stoic and steadfast. Shy and unassuming, gracious and motherly, extremely supportive. Quietly brave.
Strength	All-enduring, indomitable, stubborn and strong. Loving, loyal friend.
Weakness	Self-effacing, tendency to deny herself, insecure.
Family Members	Father: Andranik Tigranian Mother: Siranush Tigranian Sister (older): Arousiak Tigranian
Introduced in	*Qualify*
Appears in	All novels, *Aeson Black.*

Profile and Facts

Hasmik Tigranian is Gwen's friend, met during Qualification.

Hasmik is an Armenian American sixteen-year-old girl from Boston, having originally immigrated to the United States from

Yerevan, Armenia with her family when she was an eight-year-old child. She is highly skilled at knitting and crochet, very quick with her hands, and, as a result, she becomes very proficient with the Yellow Quadrant Weapons, Nets and Cords.

She is assigned to Yellow Quadrant Dorm Eight, and ends up Gwen's dormitory neighbor, with her bed adjacent to Gwen's, while Laronda's bed is on Gwen's other side.

Despite sleeping right next to Gwen all those nights, Hasmik is only introduced four days later. She has an injured ankle, bruised and swollen, which she wraps in a bandage daily, and takes pain pills, in order to continue the brutal Qualification training—which amazes Gwen and Laronda. That morning Hasmik eats breakfast with them for the first time.

During the Yellow Quadrant punishment session at the Arena Commons, Hasmik is ordered to stand on her one injured foot by an unwitting Aeson, and she faints from the pain, even while Gwen attempts to help her.

Her resolve, stoic endurance, and strength are so impressive that Xelio Vekahat notices her for the first time during that incident. While he convinces Aeson not to Disqualify Gwen, he also starts to watch Hasmik closely, especially her caring interactions with Gwen and the others.

When Gwen has to demonstrate her vocal ability to raise a shuttle before Aeson and other witnesses, Hasmik gives Gwen her own water bottle to help her parched throat.

Going into the Semi-Finals, Hasmik ranks #5,023 at RQC-3, and picks Dallas for her competition arena.

Hasmik earns 106 Final Points at the NQC, Section Fourteen, and is assigned to Team USA 14D in the Finals.

She Qualifies and ends up on Ark-Ship 809 with Dawn and Laronda, where she chooses Civilian for her life choice, and is assigned to Yellow Quadrant, Residential Deck Four Dormitory.

Once on Atlantis, Civilian Hasmik gets a job in the manufacturing sector with defense textiles, a military industry, which requires non-disclosure and a clearance. Her workplace is in the warehouse district of Nuabuut, south of Poseidon city center. With her connections, she is able to procure a special hover-vest for Blayne to use at Gwen's Wedding.

Hasmik relentlessly supports Gwen during her Games training, and also develops a warm friendship with Manala whom she assists with her cat Khemji.

At the Imperial Wedding, Xelio asks Hasmik to dance with him, but she refuses him repeatedly, which only serves to intrigue him further. Hasmik is the one woman who represents Xelio's secret ideal. Neither flashy nor strikingly beautiful, she is the opposite of flirtatious. But just like her friend Gwen, Hasmik is indomitable, strong and *real*—in her own, warm, and genuine way. Hasmik's subtle dignity, her humility and selfless caring for everyone around her, deeply touches Xelio's heart.

During the alien war, Hasmik also accompanies Manala on her final *astroctadra* Helios system mission on War-6, for moral support.

When War-6 is destroyed, Hasmik, Manala, Xelio, and many others end up marooned in space.

Unlike her companions (who managed to get on board a partially damaged, small ship), Hasmik floats all alone in space, with only a propulsion pack and her helmet comms to guide her.

In the process of weaving a safety net to help the others, her suit is torn by sharp debris and develops a slow leak. She tells no one, since there is nothing that can be done (Xelio is unable to get her on board the damaged airlock of the *depet*), and she doesn't want to distress her friends for nothing. This is when Xelio starts to reveal his true feelings for her, in desperation and grief.

Hasmik, a civilian, single-handedly and bravely saves everyone in their *depet*, and then quietly dies (before being brought back by the *pegasei* aliens).

Once Hasmik is rescued, safely hospitalized, and gets to share a room with Erita, Xelio rushes to see them. He and Hasmik finally give in to their mutual feelings for each other (and drive Erita crazy with their displays of sentiment).

In the end, Hasmik earns a black armband of Honor in recognition of her heroic act of saving Manala, George, Consul Denu,

Xelio, Command Pilot Uru Onophris, and the others, during that critical space mission.

Gwen and Aeson name their youngest daughter "Erita Hasmik," honoring both of their valiant friends.

Laronda Aimes

Role	Gwen's Friend
Eye Color	Hazel
Hair Color	Brown with blond highlights
Height	5'6"
Nickname	'Ronda, Earth Girl (called by Anu)
Color Quadrant	Yellow
Qualification Semi-Finals Dorm	Yellow Quadrant Dorm Eight
Qualification Finals	Team USA 14C
RQC-3 Rank (out of 6,023)	#3,704
Birthdate	December 17, 2031 (Green Ghost Moon 22, 9758)
Zodiac Sign	Sagittarius
Home Planet	Earth
Physical Appearance	Slim and willowy, average height, elegant ballerina build, short relaxed hair bobbed and tinted with blond highlights, brown skin, mischievous expression.
Personality Characteristics	Outgoing and chatty, friendly, assertive, doesn't suffer fools, genuine, loves to laugh.
Strength	Inquisitive, clever, and relentlessly supportive. Courageous, dynamic, true friend.
Weakness	Goes too far with proving her point. Can be pushy.
Family Members	Father: (out of the picture) Mother: Marissa Aimes (deceased) Aunt (guardian): Janice Aimes, "Auntie Janice" Brother (younger) Jamil Aimes
Introduced in	*Qualify*
Appears in	All novels, *Aeson: Black*.

Profile and Facts

Laronda Aimes is Gwen's new best friend, and the first friend she meets during Qualification.

Laronda is a fifteen-year-old African-American girl from Buffalo, New York, where she lives with her Auntie Janice and six-year-old brother Jamil. Her mother, a single parent, died when Laronda was twelve, and Laronda and Jamil went to live with her guardian aunt who worked hard to be able to afford Laronda's ballet dance lessons.

Laronda is assigned to Yellow Quadrant Dorm Eight. She puts down her bag next to Gwen's and initiates conversation as they wait with their Dorm Leader, then picks the dormitory bed right next to Gwen (with Hasmik's bed on Gwen's other side).

From there on, Laronda and Gwen start to bond.

When Gracie stupidly dumps the stolen shuttle navigation chip in Laronda's jacket pocket, Laronda ends up being falsely accused of sabotage in the shuttle incident. Gwen and Dawn go to plead on her behalf, and Gwen ends up being accused in her place, while Laronda is acquitted and released from jail.

Going into the Semi-Finals, Laronda ranks at #3,704 at the RQC-3, and picks New York for her competition arena.

For the Finals, she earns 185 Final Points at the NQC, Section Fourteen, and is assigned to Team USA 14C, where she flies on a hoverboard through the tunnels, next to Gwen. Together they survive the flooded tunnel when Gwen boards them up with hoverboards inside a lava bubble pocket.

Laronda Qualifies, and ends up on Ark-Ship 809, together with Dawn and Hasmik, where she picks Fleet Cadet as her life choice and is assigned to the Yellow Quadrant, Navigation and Guidance, Cadet Deck Four Barracks.

Laronda earns a 67% Fleet Score at the end of the first Cadet Quantum Stream Race. Then she earns an 87% Fleet Score and ranks at #104 for her ark-ship, at the end of the second Cadet QS Race.

Anu Vei, Imperial Aide, notices Laronda in her golden dress at the Yellow Zero-G Dance, and then calls her "other Earth girl," while Laronda calls him a "troll boy."

On Atlantis, Anu and Laronda continue to bicker and exchange dramatic insults, whenever Laronda comes by with the other friends to help Gwen with her preparation for the Games, and afterwards, including at Kokayi's Parade in Sky Tangle City.

On Bride Show Day, when Gwen and her friends eat at Shesep's Bar in Fish Town, things intensify. Laronda tastes Anu's scarab beer. Anu tells her about the secret ingredients—scarabs and dung. Angry barbs fly, then Laronda and Anu tussle and exchange an unexpected kiss.

On the day of the Imperial Wedding, Gwen tells Laronda to go after Anu (who barged in on Gwen and Aeson's intimate interlude yet again and is now hiding). From there on, Laronda and Anu become a couple.

During the alien war, Laronda is deployed with the other Earth Cadets, and serves on War-1, to defend Atlantis.

Logan Sangre

Role	Gwen's First Crush and Love Interest (Ex-Boyfriend)
Eye Color	Hazel
Hair Color	Raven Black with red-brown highlights
Height	5'11"
Color Quadrant	Red
Qualification Semi-Finals Dorm	Red Quadrant Dorm One
Qualification Finals	Team USA 14A
RQC-3 Rank (out of 6,023)	#143
Birthdate	March 28, 2029 (Green Pegasus 25, 9756)
Zodiac Sign	Aries
Home Planet	Earth
Physical Appearance	Handsome, with longish, wavy hair, black with reddish-brown highlights. Olive skin, chiseled angular features, hazel-brown eyes, long dark lashes, a runner's physique.
Personality Characteristics	Smart and driven to achieve, track star athlete, honor roll student, musical with a fine voice, plays guitar. Charming, attractive, and friendly. Cool and efficient, unsentimental, no-nonsense, career-oriented. Wants to go out in a blaze of glory while serving his country.
Strength	"Beauty and brains." Secret operative for Earth Union. Highly efficient.
Weakness	Calculating and impersonal.
Family Members	Father: Richard Sangre Mother: Julie Sangre Brother (older): Jeff Sangre

Introduced in	*Qualify*
Appears in	All novels, *Aeson: Black.*

Profile and Facts

Logan Sangre is Gwen's first major crush, a seventeen-year-old senior at Mapleroad Jackson High School, and later becomes her boyfriend during Qualification.

Logan is a well-rounded, popular boy in school, a National Merit Scholar, a "mathlete," and a track star athlete, who also plays lead guitar in a band, and has his pick of girls. His most recent girlfriend is Joanie Katz, with whom he just broke up.

Gwen has had a schoolgirl crush on him for years, all from a distance, and they have never really spoken until they are at RQC-3.

Logan is also an Earth Union secret operative, originally recruited by his older brother Jeff who is in the military.

Aligned with the Red Quadrant, Logan is assigned to Red Quadrant Dorm One at Pennsylvania RQC-3.

After socializing in the Red Dorm, through Gracie, then having a meal at the Arena Commons with everyone, Logan offers to teach Gwen how to run.

It is after their track practice that Logan is there when Gwen "sings down" the falling shuttle and then saves Aeson. Logan agrees to keep it quiet and tell no one, promising to keep this a secret.

During the Qualification training, Logan tells Gwen that he likes her, and they start to "date" in secret, since the Atlantean Qualification Rules do not allow romantic relationships at the compound.

Soon after Gwen's Logos voice comes into play, Logan admits to Gwen that he is an Earth Union special operative, and then also confesses to knowing that Gwen has had a crush on him when they were back in school. At first Gwen is upset, but comes to terms with it, and then agrees to be "recruited" by him and to "observe" Aeson.

As the events develop, Logan begins to notice that there is something between Gwen and the Atlantean Aeson Kass. And he starts feeling jealousy.

At Gwen's secret birthday party at the NQC, Logan gives her his small knife as a present, something that's very dear to him, and is a former present from his brother Jeff. Later on, this knife comes in very handy during the Games.

Logan Qualifies along with Gwen and many of the others, and ends up on the same Ark-Ship AS-1109. When Gwen is transferred to ICS-2, Logan chooses to be a Fleet Cadet as his life choice and gets transferred to the Flagship ICS-1 under Commander Manakteon Resoi.

Later, Logan manages to get himself onto ICS-2 and pulls a gun on Aeson to demonstrate that Earth operatives and terrorists have infiltrated the Fleet, and to warn Aeson that there is going to be an "incident" soon.

After a tense standoff, Aeson and Logan confer, and Aeson has Logan transferred under his own command to ICS-2. There Logan is assigned to Red Quadrant, Drive and Propulsion, Cadet Deck One Barracks.

Soon, the hostage incident takes place, and Logan fights alongside Aeson against the terrorists. After the Terra Patria terrorists are defeated, Logan is assigned to work with the prisoners and to interrogate Brie Walton—at which point their complicated relationship begins.

During the Blue Zero-G Dance, Logan breaks up with Gwen after her unconscious feelings for Aeson are displayed. Logan forces Gwen to face the hard truth that she is attracted to Aeson Kassiopei.

Logan is now officially Gwen's ex-boyfriend and free to date other people.

Logan ranks at #7 at beginning of the first Cadet Quantum Stream Race, and earns a 98% Fleet Score and the #3 Rank for his ark-ship at end of the first QS Race.

He ranks at #3 at the beginning of the second QS Race, and earns a 99% Fleet Score and the #2 Rank at the end of the second QS Race.

Once on Atlantis, Fleet Cadet Logan Sangre is assigned to work at the Poseidon Central Correctional Facility. There he continues to work with various Earth prisoners.

As the primary handler for Brie Walton's interrogation, Logan conveys to Aeson and Gwen that Brie wants to make a deal. Logan convinces them to put Brie in the Games as Gwen's secret protector and ally.

After the Games, Brie is the Entrepreneur Category Champion, and as per one of her Champion Wishes, Logan has to be her "servant" for a period of three months, during which she humiliates him. All through this, Brie and Logan become romantically involved.

At the end of the alien war, when Brie plans to return to Earth, Logan decides to return also, as an Earth liaison. Gwen decides to return Logan's knife to Brie, since it would make more sense for Brie to have it.

Others

The following characters fall in the interstitial category of being neither Gwen nor Aeson's core friends. Instead, they are in Aeson's employ—his Imperial Aides—or work in another capacity on behalf of Imperial *Atlantida*, and as such, are vital to the story.

Anu Vei

Role	Aeson's Imperial Aide
Eye Color	Hazel
Hair Color	Red underneath Metallic Gold
Height	5'10"
Nickname	Troll Boy (by Laronda and Gwen)
Family Nickname	*Suk-suk* (named after *sukrat* fish)
Color Quadrant	Red
Birthdate	Green Mar-Yan 5, 9753 (May 27, 2025)
Zodiac Sign	Snow Anubawan (Jackal)
Home Planet	Atlantis
Physical Appearance	Medium height, wiry and slim, light skin and freckles. Long and lean face. Long gilded hair in a segmented tail.
Personality Characteristics	Aggravating and abrasive, blunt, with a rough sense of humor. Critical of others. Irreverent of authority. Likes to complain and play practical jokes, immature due to his upbringing. Genius-level intellect, mathematically inclined. Loyal and fiery-tempered.
Strength	Brilliant with numbers, deeply loyal to individuals who earn his respect, cannot be bought or compromised. Warm-hearted underneath his bluster.
Weakness	Insecure, overly critical of others. Poor social skills.

Family Members	Father: Bukko Vei
	Mother: Aoma Vei
	Brother (older): Mabu Vei
	Brother (younger): Refu Vei
	Sister (younger): Chirim Vei
	Brother (youngest): Kooi Vei
Introduced in	*Compete*
Appears in	*Compete, Win, Survive, Aeson: Black.*

Profile and Facts

Anu Vei (AH-NOO VEH-EE) is an Imperial Aide to Aeson and the Central Command Office (CCO). He is the second Imperial Aide after Pheret Aduo.

Anu comes from a poor family in a tiny coastal fishing village, Nifa (population of less than forty people, basically five families) on the barren shore of the Nehehatlan Ocean. When Anu is a young boy, his aptitude test shows him to be a mathematical genius (despite being illiterate), so young Aeson visits his village to recruit him for the Fleet.

The family engages in a fish fight, tremendously amusing Aeson, and Anu himself cusses him out, displaying a unique irreverence for the authority of the Imperial Kassiopei. Aeson convinces Anu's mother to part with Anu and, in exchange, the family receives a new fish barrel, a new hut, a year's supply of food and other necessities for the village.

Once in Poseidon, Anu takes remedial courses, attends evening Cadet School training, and becomes Aeson's Imperial Aide. Aeson tolerates much of his uncouth rudeness because of his irreverent honesty and because Anu makes him genuinely laugh.

Anu is aligned with the Red Quadrant.

He is first introduced in *Compete* when Gwen becomes an Imperial Aide at the CCO. Gwen finds him rude and abrasive, and Anu calls Gwen "Earth girl."

It becomes apparent that Anu insults everyone. He also calls Gennio "fat-brain," and says outrageous things to get a rise out of people.

After working together for many months, Gwen slowly becomes accustomed to his crude and immature humor and he starts to grow on her.

Anu notices Laronda for the first time in her golden dress at the Yellow Zero-G Dance, and then calls her the "other Earth girl," while Laronda calls him a "troll boy."

When Aeson chooses Gwen for his Bride, Anu has trouble believing and processing this, but eventually comes to terms that Gwen is now someone he has to respect as much as he respects Aeson.

On Atlantis, Anu and Laronda continue to bicker and exchange dramatic insults, whenever Laronda comes by with the other friends to help Gwen with her preparation for the Games, and afterwards, including at Kokayi's Parade in Sky Tangle City.

Anu helps Gwen with Games training by introducing her to Gavreel and Krui, two former criminals who teach her the hand piercing trick and other tips to give her an advantage in the games.

Together with Gennio, Anu assists Aeson with enacting the Rim, by setting up the tech needed to run the feeds that interrupt the Games streaming broadcast.

Anu also bets on Gwen during the Games, winning a lot of money.

On Bride Show Day, when Gwen and her friends eat at Shesep's Bar in Fish Town, things intensify between Anu and Laronda. Anu is outraged when Laronda grabs his pitcher and tastes Anu's scarab beer. Angry barbs fly, then Laronda and Anu tussle and exchange an unexpected kiss.

On the day of the Imperial Wedding, Laronda goes looking for Anu who hides after having barged in on Gwen and Aeson's intimate interlude yet again. From there on, Anu and Laronda become a couple.

Anu has met his fiery match.

Gennio Rukkat

Role	Aeson's Imperial Aide
Eye Color	Dark Brown
Hair Color	Metallic Gold
Height	5'11"
Nickname	Fat-brain (by Anu)
Color Quadrant	Blue
Birthdate	Yellow Pegasus 25, 9755 (August 05, 2028)
Zodiac Sign	Lightning Uum (Owl)
Home Planet	Atlantis
Physical Appearance	Thick-set, dark brown skin, short, tightly curling, gilded hair. Pleasant face with blunt chin and flattened nose. Tenor voice.
Personality Characteristics	Mild-mannered, calm, polite and kind. Technically oriented, good with details, smart and studious.
Strength	Detail oriented, hard-working, kind and helpful.
Weakness	Uncertain, absentminded, does not take the initiative unless instructed.
Family Members	Father: Fiomi Rukkat Mother: Laksati Rukkat Sister (older): Jeina Rukkat Brother (older): Hanzu Rukkat
Introduced in	*Compete*
Appears in	*Compete, Win, Survive, Aeson: Black.*

Profile and Facts

Gennio Rukkat (GEH-NEE-OH ROOK-KAH-T) is an Imperial Aide to Aeson and the Central Command Office (CCO). He is the third Imperial Aide to be hired after Pheret Aduo and Anu Vei.

Gennio is aligned with the Blue Quadrant. He comes from an affluent but not noble family in Poseidon.

He is first introduced in *Compete* when he helps Gwen with settling in. He also takes Gwen to the Observation Deck to observe the Mars orbit pass, since he has an interest in astronomy and is visually documenting the Fleet journey. This is when Trey Smith and Brie Walton make fun of him, which he does not notice.

In advance of the Blue Zero-G Dance, Gennio sends his friend Vazara Hotat (who serves as the Music Mage for several Dances) to help Gwen out in the trend and fashion department.

When they arrive on Atlantis and land, Gennio is the one to tell Gwen, "Welcome to Atlantis."

Together with Anu, he is also quite confused when Gwen reveals to them that she has been chosen by Aeson as the Imperial Bride. However, he comes to terms with it much more quickly than Anu.

Gennio is in charge of gadgets, and on Aeson's orders, gets Gwen a PCDU, or as she calls it, a "wrist thingie."

At the Imperial Wedding, Gennio dances with Gwen's friend and Pilot Partner Chiyoko. He also socializes with Chiyoko at the Green Zero-G Dance.

Consul Suval Denu

Role	Imperial Consul, Diplomat, ACA Liaison, Gwen's Court Protocol Instructor
Eye Color	Dark Brown
Hair Color	Bald (before, dark brown), Gold Wigs
Height	5'7"
Color Quadrant	Green
Birthdate	Yellow Ghost Moon 9, 9725 (March 6, 1990)
Zodiac Sign	Magnetic Shuut (Feather)
Home Planet	Atlantis
Physical Appearance	Slim, slight, middle-aged man, warm suntan skin. Oval, lean and elegant face, brows painted lapis lazuli blue over black, austere lips, completely bald underneath grand gilded wigs; wears extravagant robes, jewelry, and is perfectly manicured and made-up.
Personality Characteristics	Musical tenor voice, delicate timbre. Impeccably polite, perfectly versed in Court Protocol and politics. Fashion and cosmetics expert. Deceptive chameleon persona, can seem servile and full of adulation toward the Imperials while haughty and capricious toward lesser rank. Foppish and extravagant. Gracious, warm, and astute underneath the courtly veneer. Highly intelligent. A matchmaker.
Strength	Expert in Court Protocol and diplomacy, subtle and perceptive, wise, intelligent, analytical, conciliatory, kind and helpful.
Weakness	Plays the chameleon too well, does not permit his true personality to reveal itself. Self-repressive. Secretly insecure about his noble status.

Family Members	Father: Huonat Denu, Lord (deceased) Mother: Lucaira Denu, Lady Sister (younger): Jolura Adraegi Nephew: Uxuti Adraegi Niece: Nebnaida Adraegi
Introduced in	*Compete*
Appears in	*Compete, Win, Survive, Aeson: Black.*

Profile and Facts

Suval Denu (Soo-VAH-L DEH-Noo), commonly referred to as Consul Denu, is a skilled diplomat, Imperial Consul, and ACA Liaison on the Earth Mission. He is also an IEC Member, and a noble courtier, fourth generation, Low Court.

Despite his extensive preoccupation with his own family tree, Consul Denu's family is considered recent nobility, and at this point Denu is the last of his line, with no offspring prospects except for his sister's children. Unless his personal situation changes, he will transfer his Rank and inheritance to them.

Suval Denu is highly educated, a connoisseur of the arts and is extremely well read. His chameleon personality hides the subtlety of a poet and the steely mind of a diplomat.

Suval Denu first appears in *Compete* as an extravagant, petulant, and foppish courtier who has been asked by Aeson to tutor Gwen in Imperial Court Protocol. For that reason, he is transferred from the flagship ICS-1 to ICS-2.

Denu's main role on the Earth Mission is as an Imperial Consul, a diplomatic liaison with Earth governments. Gwen is not aware that his role as her tutor is performed as a special favor for the Crown Prince.

During the many months of the journey, Consul Denu pays close attention to Gwen and Aeson interacting together and comprehends that there is a budding relationship involved. He also realizes that Gwen is good for Aeson, and he helps her with subtle advice and mentorship during his Court Protocol classes, and then with actual fashion and makeup for the Red and Yellow Zero-G Dances. Denu sends his young assistant Kem to perform a high-end makeover for Gwen, and he even lends her some expensive jewelry to be used strategically to entice Aeson.

Just before arrival on Atlantis, Aeson partially confides in Consul Denu and engages his services when he makes his bold plans to make Gwen his Bride. Denu is in charge of making Gwen ready for the Imperial Court on that fateful evening of the Assembly.

After she officially becomes the chosen Imperial Bride, Denu formally enters Gwen's measurements in the Imperial Book of Fashion. From there on, he handles various aspects of Gwen's appearance and professional fashion choices. And he plays a wonderful role in assisting her with a variety of other Courtly duties and formal events leading up to the Imperial Wedding.

In addition to assisting Gwen, Consul Denu is of great help to others such as the Imperatris Devora, and Princess Manala who finds great comfort in Denu's presence. He even bonds with Charles Lark.

During the alien war, Consul Denu accompanies Manala on the two *astroctadra* missions to lend his support, and ends up marooned in space alongside the others, until rescued.

Consul Denu also recommends that George Lark get a diplomatic position with the IEC, because he recognizes George's talents in that regard.

To show Consul Denu their appreciation, Gwen and Aeson name one of their sons "Suval Gordon" after him.

Character Groups and Categories

The following are simple lists of characters as introduced (in order of appearance, or first mention) in the four core books of the series: *Qualify, Compete, Win,* and *Survive.* Additional characters from the novellas *Aeson: Blue* and *Aeson: Black* are also included.

The characters are also grouped into some meaningful categories for ease of reference.

Earthlings

Lark Family

Gwen Lark
Margot Lark
George Lark
Charles Lark
Gordie Lark
Gracie Lark

Students and Faculty from Mapleroad Jackson Middle and High School and elsewhere in Vermont

Students

Carrie Willis
Mindy Erikson
Nick Warren
Ann Finnbar
Gary Abbott
Nancy Andrew
Mark Gardner
Jenny Hawls
Chris Jasper
Jeremy Carverson
Logan Sangre
Joanie Katz*
Mindy Clarence
Josh Merrow*
Eddie
Archer Richards
Blayne Dubois

Faculty

Mrs. Grayland
Ms. Wayne
Mrs. Bayard
Principal Marksen

Others (Government and Media)

President Katherine Donahue
Bill Anderson
Cathy Estrada

Pennsylvania Regional Qualification Center (RQC) 3

Gina Curtis
Jaideep "Jai" Bhagat
Mateo Perez
Janice Quinn
Claudia Grito
Laronda Aimes
John Nicolard
Mark Foster
Theresa
Jack Carell
Chris
Mr. Warrenson
Wade Ruthers
Olivia
Tremaine Walters
Joshua Bell
Ashley
Charlie Venice
Daniel Tover
Mia Weston
Becca Marlin
Dionte Jones
Derek Sunder
Jessica Conlett
Dawn Williams
Greg Chee
Antwon Marks
Hasmik Tigranian
Amy Calver
Erin Tsai
Roy Tsai
Ken Fisher

Isabella Saltwater
Samuel Duarte
Kadeem Cantrell
Craig Beller
Desiree Bell
Jaime Robles
Mamraj Shahad

New York RQC-1 (Televised)

Jimmy Wong
Angela Manwell

Qualification Semi-Finals, Los Angeles

Gwen Lark
Sarah Thornwald
Jared Holder
Zoe Blatt
Ethan Jamerson
Kadeem Cantrell
Grace Lark

National Qualification Center (NQC), Colorado

(new characters only)
Carlos Villa
Shontae Smith
Annie
Blair

Qualification Finals

(new characters only)
Emilio Flores
Jack

Earth Refugees (COMPETE)

Gwen Lark
Grace Lark
Gordon Lark
Charles and Margot Lark (originally left on Earth)
George Nestor Lark (originally left on Earth)
Logan Sangre
Adriana Regalo
Jennica Tulls
Lars Hansen
Alla Vetrova
Trey Smith
Brie Walton
Hugo Moreno
Erin Tsai
Roy Tsai
Kadeem Cantrell
Blayne Dubois
Laronda Aimes
Dawn Williams
Hasmik Tigranian
Daniel Tover
Jenny
Chiyoko Sato
Conrad Hart
Leopold Deller
DeeDee Kim
Oliver Parker
Leon Madongo
Marc Goldstein

Earth Refugees (WIN)

Gwen Lark
Grace Lark
Gordon Lark
Blayne Dubois
Dawn Williams
Hasmik Tigranian
Chiyoko Sato
Laronda Aimes
Logan Sangre
Gabriella (Brie) Walton
George Lark**
Charles Lark**
Margot Lark**

** Indicates their appearance only in hallucinations.

Earthlings (SURVIVE)

Gwen Lark
Brie Walton
Grace Lark
Gordon Lark
Charles Lark
George Lark
Margot Lark*
Laronda Aimes
Hasmik Tigranian
Blayne Dubois
Dawn Williams
Chiyoko Sato
Logan Sangre
Yana Svoboda
Li Jie
Claudia Grito
Darius Harrod

Other Earthlings Mentioned (SURVIVE)

US President Katherine Donahue*
King William of England*
British Prime Minister Corwell*
Chinese President Liu Kai Wong*
United Industan President Ghatak*
Russian President Zabrodov*

Atlanteans

Atlanteans (QUALIFY)

Commander Manakteon Resoi
Ligerat Faroi
Oalla Keigeri
Nefir Mekei
Keruvat (Ker) Ruo
Aeson Kassiopei (Kass)
Xelio (Xel) Vekahat
Chiar Nuridat*
Felekamen Gori*
Tiliar Vahad*
Erita (Eri) Qwas
Lirama Rikat
Mikelion Wasi
Qurume Ateni
Ekit Jei
Radra Vilai

Atlanteans (COMPETE)

Aeson Kassiopei
Manakteon Resoi
Bequa Larei
Keruvat Ruo
Erita Qwas
Oalla Keigeri
Xelio Vekahat
Gennio Rukkat
Anu Vei
Tahirah Zulei*
Mithrat Okoi
Lady Tirinea "Tiri" Fuorai
Nilara Gradat
Baritei Gato
Consul Suval Denu
Kem
Quarar Ritazet*
Chior Kla
Klavit Xotoi
Vazara Hotat
Miwat
Romhutat Kassiopei

Atlanteans (WIN)

Aeson Kassiopei
Romhutat Kassiopei
Lady Tirinea "Tiri" Fuorai
Consul Suval Denu
Anu Vei
Gennio Rukkat
Devora Kassiopei
Manala Kassiopei
Deneb Gratu
Tiamat "Thalassa" Irtiu
Hedj "The White Bird" Kukkait
Manakteon Resoi
Desher Keigeri
Lady Hathora Sekru
Lady Zua Kainaat
Lady Irana Nokut
Elikara Vekahat*
Aranit Liwei
Kem
Oalla Keigeri
Keruvat Ruo
Xelio Vekahat
Lord Arao Hetepheret
Dame Tammuz Akten
Thebet Obwai
Tiago Guu
Buhaat Hippeis*
Erita Qwas
Gavreel
Krui
Pheret Aduo*
Rovat Bennu*

Takhat*
Hijep Tiofon*
Shirahtet*
Lady Ishtar Sitamun*
Lord Asiwet*
Amasis*
Gobu*
Lady Iela Nastasen*
Nefir Mekei*
Sarpanit Latao
Ujaste Naat
Tamira Bedut*
Futo
Maga
The man in the golden mask, The Rim
Zaap Guvai
Chihar Agwath
Larahat Sei
Kokayi Jeet
Oshaharat Feveh
Lolu Eetatu
Khadram Eetatu
Fadut
Xofati
Vidam
Kateb Nuletat
Tuar Momet
Avaneh Lehatut
Fawzi Boto
Rurim Kiv
Sofia Veforoi
Mirin*
Leetana Chipuo
Ukou Dwetat

Atlanteans (SURVIVE)

Aeson Kassiopei
Romhutat Kassiopei
Nefir Mekei
Quoni Enutat
Hirat Sumbui
Devora Kassiopei
Oalla Keigeri
Erita Qwas
Keruvat Ruo
Xelio Vekahat
Manala Kassiopei
Anu Vei
Gennio Rukkat
Areviktet Heru
Hijep Tiofon
Shirahtet Kuruam
Consul Suval Denu
Kephasa Sewu
Miramis Opu
Rovat Bennu
Desher Keigeri
Hedj "The White Bird" Kukkait
Kateb Nuletat
Kokayi Jeet
Lolu Eetatu
Chihar Agwath
Rea Bunit
Leetana Chipuo
Mineb Inei
Rurim Kiv
Sofia Veforoi
Fawzi Boto

Ukou Dwetat

Tamira Bedut

Therutat Nuudri

Lady Isulat

Aranit Liwei

Darumet Azai

Tuar Momet

Yeraz Nuletat

Mamai-Jeet

Tiago Guu

Buhaat Hippeis

Reporters asking questions during Bridal Media Event, media outlets:

Free Poseidon News

News of the Golden Bay

The Daily Bay Flow

Talk and Laugh News Digest

Eos News Feed

Contemporary Court Style and Gossip

Bay City News and Entertainment

Kem

Dame Tammuz Akten

Lady Carilla Oruvi

Lady Godun Yator

Lady Iskandrat Suriner

First Lady Aduar Vekahat

Lady Ghara Vekahat

First Lady Kuz Ruo

Lady Tirinea "Tiri" Fuorai

First Lady Vahiz Fuorai

Lord Fuorai

Lady Zua Kainaat

Lady Hathora Sekru

Lady Irana Nokut

Rertu*

Manakteon Resoi*

Igara Cvutu

Semiram*
Semmi*
Arlenari Kassiopei*
Eodea Tecpatl
Radanthet Ulumaq
Danaat*
Evandros
Anen Qur
Inevar Arelik
Osuo Menbuut
Wilem Paeh
Duu Valam
Qedeh Adamer
Shesep
Amaiar Uluatl
Culuar Efrebu
Nergal Duha
Hesper Kassiopei*
Etamharat Kassiopei*
Ter Uxmal
Lord Tutanamat Argosaen
First Lady Irumala Argosaen
Asclep
Saramana Zhar
Cretheo
Amasis
Saiva Neidos
Takhat
Muutat Bisfuri*
Churu Kassiopei*
Narmeradat Kassiopei*
Merneit Kassiopei*
Enhuvarat
Selmiris Teth
Uru Onophris

Axela Buiri
Xurut Ralafu
Oron Kassiopei*
Inevar Arelik
Duu Valam
Bakar Ramajet
Valel Siduaz
Lafaoh Ungreb
Lord Arao Hetepheret
Babi
Nepht
Sheolaat Heru
Chudo Batiaxaat
Selmiris Teth
Mayavat Meropei
Various unnamed staff at Phoinios Heights estate
Various unnamed palace staff
Various unnamed *Astra Daimon*
Various unnamed Pilots in the SPC
Various unnamed members of the IEC
Various unnamed SPC Special Forces Members
Margot Arlenari Kassiopei*
Romhutat "Rommi" Charles Kassiopei*
Suval "Suvi" Gordon Kassiopei*
Oalla Ann Kassiopei*
Erita Hasmik Kassiopei*

The Games of the Atlantis Grail

Top Ten Champions

Rank	Name	Category	Final Points
1.	Kokayi Jeet	Entertainer	60,479
2.	Hedj Kukkait	Warrior	46,291
3.	Kateb Nuletat	Inventor	6,137
4.	Leetana Chipuo	Animal Handler	5,804
5.	Rurim Kiv	Artist	4,107
6.	Gwen Lark	Vocalist	3,972
7.	Brie Walton	Entrepreneur	3,821
8.	Mineb Inei	Technician	3,605
9.	Ukou Dwetat	Athlete	3,428
10.	Rea Bunit	Scientist	3,394

Team Lark

Gwen Lark – Vocalist
Zaap Guvait – Animal Handler
Chihar Agwath – Scientist
Brie Walton – Entrepreneur
Kokayi Jeet – Entertainer
Lolu Eetatu – Technician
Tuar Momet – Athlete
Avaneh Lehatut – Warrior
Kateb Nuletat – Inventor
(Note: there is no Artist on Team Lark)

Other Contenders

Deneb Gratu
Tiamat "Thalassa" Irtiu
Hedj "The White Bird" Kukkait
Sarpanit Latao
Ujaste Naat
Larahat Sei
Oshaharat Feveh
Khadram Eetatu
Fadut
Xofati
Vidam
Fawzi Boto
Rurim Kiv
Sofia Veforoi
Leetana Chipuo
Mineb Inei
Rea Bunit
Ukou Dwetat

Other Character Groups

Media Personalities

Games Related Media

Tiago Guu, Host of *Grail Games Daily*
Buhaat Hippeis, Host of *Winning the Grail*
Futo, Pre-Games Trials
Maga, Pre-Games Trials
The man in the golden mask, "The Rim"
Various Games announcers

Other Media

Desher Keigeri, news anchor for Helios-Ra Imperial Poseidon Network (HRIPN)
Reporters asking questions during Bridal Media Event on behalf of media outlets:
Free Poseidon News
News of the Golden Bay
The Daily Bay Flow
Talk and Laugh News Digest
Eos News Feed
Contemporary Court Style and Gossip
Bay City News and Entertainment

Earth Organizations

Earth Union – Military special operational unit sanctioned by the United Nations to infiltrate Atlantean Society and Fleet to gain knowledge of Atlantean technology and resources to benefit Earth.

Known Members:

Brie Walton
Logan Sangre
Daniel Tover
Jeff Sangre

Terra Patria – Terrorist group formed to remove Atlantean influence.

Known Members

Trey Smith
Brie Walton (undercover)
Jenny

Sunset Alliance – Terrorist group formed to remove Atlantean influence.

Atlantean Organizations

Atlantis Central Agency (ACA) – Established by Imperator Romhutat Kassiopei as a liaison agency between Earth and Atlantis. ACA Director Hijep Tiofon

Science and Technology Agency (STA)
STA Director Rovat Bennu

Legal and Correctional Agency (LCA)
Arch Corrector Peleset Frawei (not mentioned by name)

Poseidon Central Correctional Facility
Warden (not mentioned by name)
Mafdet (goddess of law and punishment, basis of justice system, not mentioned)

Correctors – General police force on Atlantis; military police with primary duties in the Fleet; civilian police with primary duties in Imperial *Atlantida.*

Imperial Executive Council (IEC) – Branch of Government designed to offset and balance the power of the Imperator.

The Imperial Executive Council

Imperator Romhutat Kassiopei
Imperial Fleet Commander Manakteon Resoi
Imperial Crown Prince Aeson Kassiopei
Consul Suval Denu
Lord Arao Hetepheret
Dame Tammuz Akten
Lady Ishtar Sitamun
Lord Asiwet
Council Member Amasis
Council Member Gobu
Lady Iela Nastasen
Council Member Takhat
First Priest Shirahtet
ACA Director Hijep Tiofon
STA Director Rovat Bennu
Various unspecified members from Atlantis Central Agency (ACA)
and Science and Technology Agency (STA).

IEC Members According to Political Positions

Member	Political Position
Everyone	Mobilize the Fleet.
Imperator Council Member Takhat First Priest Shirahtet ACA Director Hijep Tiofon	Keep it all secret from the public.
Lord Arao Hetepheret Dame Tammuz Akten	Quickly select and train the best Earth Cadets for Star Pilot Corps duty.
Lord Asiwet	Tell the general public of Atlantis about the alien threat.
Lady Ishtar Sitamun	Tell the Earth refugees about the alien threat and keep it secret from the public.
Council Member Amasis	Deploy Atlantean-only forces; was anti-Earth mission.
Council Member Gobu	Increase and improve monitoring surveillance for aliens; listen for them via sensitive sound equipment; look for them in the skies, underneath the oceans.
Lord Arao Hetepheret Dame Tammuz Akten	Comply with the aliens' demands. *(The Imperator emphatically says "no;" cannot comply; they want to limit our technology.)*
Lady Iela Nastasen	Prepare for possible evacuation from Atlantis; escape again to the stars; search for suitable new planet far away.
ACA Director Hijep Tiofon	Return to Earth to pick up more people and resources before the

	asteroid hits. Earth UN might be an ally.
Aeson Kassiopei	Pool the resources of Earth and Atlantis against the common enemy.

Various Priesthood Members

Therutat Nuudri, First Priestess of Amrevet-Ra, The Venerable One
Lady Isulat, Priestess of Amrevet-Ra
Darumet Azai, First Priest of Amrevet-Ra, The Venerable One
Shirahtet Kuruam, First Priest of Kassiopei

Fleet and Military

Helios System Station Nomarchs and SPC Commanders

Atlas Station
Station Nomarch **Dythrat**
War-1 – Command Pilot **Manakteon Resoi** (Imperial *Atlantida*)
War-2 – Command Pilot **Amaiar Uluatl** (New Deshret)

Olympos Station
Station Nomarch **Yelen**
War-3 – Command Pilot **Chudo Batiaxaat** (Ubasti)
War-4 – Command Pilot **Saiva Neidos** (Eos-Heket)

Atlantis Station / Star Pilot Corps Headquarters
Station Nomarch **Evandros**
War-5 – Command Pilot **Selmiris Teth** (Vai Naat)
War-6 – Command Pilot **Uru Onophris** (Ptahleon)

Ishtar Station
Station Nomarch **Danaat**
War-7 – Command Pilot **Mayavat Meropei** (Shuria)

Tammuz Station
Station Nomarch **Cretheo**
War-8 – Command Pilot **Lafaoh Ungreb** (Bastet)

Septu Station
Station Nomarch **Asclep**
War-9 – Command Pilot **Saramana Zhar** (Qurartu)

Rah Station
Station Nomarch **Rertu**
War-10 – Command Pilot **Eodea Tecpatl** (Ankh-Tawi, Weret, combined forces)

Pegasus Retrieval Team (PRT)

Captain Valel Siduaz – SPC Special Forces; assigned to Gwen's PRT for the Khenneb Mission.

Six Shìrén Cadet Pilots (Ankhurat)

Blayne Dubois
Brie Walton
Claudia Grito
Darius Harrod
Li Jie
Yana Svoboda

Astroctadra Missions

Ghost Moon Mission

Mission Coordinate #1: Mar Yan (moon).
Logos Voice User: **Gwen Lark**
Fighter Ship: *Khepri*
Flight Team:
    Gwen Lark
    Oalla Keigeri
    Axela Buiri
    Xurut Ralafu

Mission Coordinate #2: Amrevet (moon).
Logos Voice User: **Aeson Kassiopei**
Fighter Ship: *Mafdet*
Flight Team:
    Aeson Kassiopei (Solo)
    Additional personnel waiting on the moon.

Mission Coordinate #3: Atlantis (The Atlantis Grail Stadium).
Logos Voice User: **Imperator Romhutat Kassiopei**

Mission Coordinate #4: Pegasus (moon).
Logos Voice User: **Gordie Lark**
Fighter Ship: *Khepri*
Flight Team:
    Gordie Lark
    Erita Qwas
    Two Fleet Crew (unnamed)

Mission Coordinate #5: Atlantis high orbit.
Logos Voice User: **Manala Kassiopei**
Fighter Ship: Battle Barge (War-5)

Flight Team:
    Manala Kassiopei
    Command Pilot Selmiris Teth
    George Lark
    Xelio Vekahat
    Consul Suval Denu
    Various Fleet Crew

Mission Coordinate #6: Atlantis high orbit.
Logos Voice User: **Anen Qur**, First Speaker of the Ennead of Ubasti,
Fighter Ship: Battle Barge (War-6)
Flight Team:
    Anen Qur
    Command Pilot Uru Onophris
    Keruvat Ruo
    Various Fleet Crew

Helios System Astroctadra Mission

Mission Coordinate: Perpendicular to Helios orbital plane (below)
Logos Voice User: **Gwen Lark**
Fighter Ship: Battle Barge (War-2)
Flight Team:
    Gwen Lark
    Erita Qwas
    Command Pilot Amaiar Uluatl of New Deshret

Mission Coordinate: Perpendicular to Helios orbital plane (above)
Logos Voice User: **Manala Kassiopei**
Fighter Ship: Battle Barge (War-6)
Flight Team:
    Manala Kassiopei,
    Hasmik Tigranian
    Xelio Vekahat
    George Lark
    Consul Suval Denu

Command Pilot Uru Onophris of Ptahleon

Mission Coordinate: Rah
Logos Voice User: **Sheolaat Heru**
Fighter Ship: Battle Barge (War-5)
Flight Team:
    Princess Sheolaat Heru of New Deshret
    Command Pilot Selmiris Teth of Vai Naat

Mission Coordinate: Septu
Logos Voice User: **Anen Qur**
Fighter Ship: Battle Barge (War-3)
Flight Team:
Anen Qur, First Speaker of the Ennead of Ubasti
Command Pilot Chudo Batiaxaat of Ubasti

Mission Coordinate: Tammuz
Logos Voice User: **Gordie Lark**
Fighter Ship: Battle Barge (War-8)
Flight Team:
    Gordie Lark
    Oalla Keigeri
    Charles Lark (with Margot's urn)
    Command Pilot Lafaoh Ungreb of Bastet

Mission Coordinate: Ishtar
Logos Voice User: **Aeson Kassiopei**
Fighter Ship: Battle Barge (War-7, *Depet-Ra* with Commander on board.)
Flight Team:
    Aeson Kassiopei
    Keruvat Ruo
    Anu Vei
    Gennio Rukkat
    Command Pilot Mayavat Meropei of Shuria

Non-Human Others

Aliens
Arion *(Win, Survive)*
Various unnamed *pegasei (Win, Survive)*
"They" ancient enemy aliens *(Compete, Win, Survive)*

Cats
Khemji *(Win, Survive)*
Samantha* *(Survive)*

"They" Aliens (Ancient Gods)

The mysterious "They" aliens are mentioned in *Compete* and *Win*, and finally arrive on stage in *Survive*. They appear as trans-dimensional spheres of light and then take on vaguely humanoid form. Meanwhile, the deadly OSIRIS spheres of light are revealed to be automated, non-sentient technology.

Thoth
Isis
Horus
Set
OSIRIS

The Atlantean Zodiac

Introducing, the Atlantean Zodiac! The stars and constellations around the colony planet Atlantis are completely different, so of course their version of astrology is completely different as well.

Atlanteans don't bother to use astrology to predict the future, only to understand the psychology of personality types and interactions.

Below is a handy basic chart of all the main astrological signs. The personality types, character interpretations, compatibility matches, and other details are beyond the scope of this volume.

If you want to learn more and discover your own Atlantean Zodiac Sign, see *The Atlantis Grail Zodiac*, a separate book that covers this subject in-depth.

16 Signs of the Atlantean Zodiac

Order	Element / Sign	Symbol	Month
1	Void Bakriku	Vulture	Green Amrevet
2	Ice Astroctadra	Four-Point Star	Green Pegasus
3	Snow Anubawan	Jackal	Green Mar-Yan
4	Water Miewu	Cat	Green Ghost Moon
5	Vapor Leontar	Lion	Red Amrevet
6	Air Sebeku	Crocodile	Red Pegasus
7	Smoke Sesemet	Horse	Red Mar-Yan
8	Fire Delphit	Dolphin	Red Ghost Moon
9	Magmatic Draguos	Dragon	Yellow Amrevet
10	Lightning Uum	Owl	Yellow Pegasus
11	Electric Aixi	Swan	Yellow Mar-Yan
12	Magnetic Shuut	Feather	Yellow Ghost Moon
13	Radiant Kheprio	Scarab	Blue Amrevet
14	Gravity Uraeus	Serpent	Blue Pegasus
15	Quantum Depet	Boat	Blue Mar-Yan
16	Starlight Akhet	Horizon	Blue Ghost Moon

Dramatis Personae

(Complete Character List in Alphabetical Order)

A

Abaivara (AH-BAH-Y-VAH-RAH) – *astra daimon* at Aeson's *astra daimon* initiation ceremony; appears in *Aeson: Black*.

Adriana Regalo – Qualified Candidate on board Ark-Ship 1109 (Gwen's original ship); chooses Civilian and is assigned to the Red Quadrant, Residential Deck One Dormitory; Appears in *Compete*.

Aduar Vekahat (AH-DOO-AHR VEH-KAH-HAH-T) – First Lady of House Vekahat; 109th generation, High Court; from Southern Uru Province; Xelio's mother; introduced to Gwen at the Ladies of the Court Bridal event; appears in *Survive*, mentioned in *Aeson: Blue*.

Aeson Kass (Earth) / **Aeson Kassiopei** (Atlantis) (AY-SUN KASS / AH-EH-SOHN KAH-SEE-OH-PAY) – see Major Characters.

Aeva* (AH-EH-VAH) – Erita Qwas's younger sister; mentioned in *Aeson: Blue*.

Alla Vetrova – Qualified Candidate transferred (on the same shuttle with Gwen) from Ark-Ship 1109 to ICS-2; assigned to Blue Quadrant, Network Systems, Cadet Deck Two Barracks; partnered with Conrad Hart in Pilot Training and QS Races; ranks #1 at the beginning of the first Cadet Quantum Stream Race; earns 100% and ranks #1 at the end of the first QS Race; Ranks #1 at the beginning of the second QS Race; Earns 100% and ranks #1 (champion) at the end of the second QS Race; appears in *Compete*.

Amaiar Uluatl (AH-MAH-EE-YAHR OOH-LOO-AHT-L) – SPC Command Pilot assigned to War-2 (carrying Gwen to her final mission coordinate); Commander of the Pharikonei Fleet from New Deshret; majority of officers and crew of War-2 from New Deshret; killed when War-2 is destroyed in a plasma jet ejected from the star Helios during the Helios System final *astroctadra* mission; appears in *Survive*.

Amasis (AH-MAH-SEE-S) – Member of the Imperial Executive Council (IEC); political position: deploy Atlantean-only forces to fight the alien enemy; is staunchly against the Earth mission; mentioned in *Win*, appears in *Survive*.

Amy Calver – Candidate, assigned to Green Dorm Eleven at the Pennsylvania RQC-3; George's friend (possibly romantic); appears in *Qualify*.

Anen Qur (AH-NEN KOOR) – the First Speaker of the Ennead of Ubasti; has the Logos Voice; participates in both the *astroctadra* missions, first one on War-6, second one on War-3; appears in *Survive*.

Angela Manwell – Candidate who ranks #7 at New York RQC-1; shown on TV during the Qualification Semi-Finals media broadcast; appears in *Qualify*.

Ann Finnbar – student at Mapleroad Jackson High School; Gwen's best friend at school, her first BFF; Gwen names her second daughter "Oalla Ann" after her; appears in *Qualify*, mentioned in *Compete*, hallucinated in *Win*.

Annie – Candidate who occupies bunk next to Gwen at the NQC; member of Team USA 14 during Qualification Finals, letter assignment unknown; appears in *Qualify*.

Antwon Marks – Candidate assigned to Yellow Quadrant Dorm Eight at Pennsylvania RQC-3; partners with Gwen in Mr. Warrenson's Atlantean Tech class, has perfect pitch; appears in *Qualify*.

Anu Vei (AH-NOO VEH-EE) – see Major Characters.

Aranit Liwei (AH-RAH-NEET LEE-WEH-EE) – Gwen's personal maid at the Imperial Palace; has an attitude at first; appears in *Win, Survive*.

Arao Hetepheret (AH-RAH-OH HEH-TEH-FEH-REH-T) – Lord of House Hetepheret; Member of the Imperial Executive Council (IEC); Reform Faction of IEC; political position: Atlantis should comply with the aliens' demands, meanwhile, quickly select and train the best Earth Cadets for Star Pilot Corps duty; worn-faced, river-red clay skin; appears in *Win, Survive*.

Archer Richards – student at Mapleroad Jackson High School who slips from his hoverboard but hangs on, showing tenacity; appears in *Qualify*.

Areviktet Heru (AH-REH-VEEK-TEHT HEH-ROO) – the Pharikon of New Deshret, ruling equivalent of Imperator; similar to the Kassiopei, descendant of an original ancient Atlantean Family on Earth; very elderly but sharp; appears in *Survive*.

Arion (AH-REE-OHN) – Trans-dimensional sentient alien being of a species known as *pegasei* (singular, *pegasus*); a name given by Gwen to the alien so that she can refer to him/her/it; works with Gwen during Stage Four of the Games after she learns the secret to communicating with the *pegasei*; takes the forms of a dolphin, traditional winged mythological horse known as a Pegasus on Earth, and a cheetah; released from bondage by Gwen at the end of the Triathlon Race; takes on the miniaturized shape of the Great Sphinx of Giza; guides Gwen to comprehend Starlight; (with other *pegasei*) saves Erita and Hasmik; (with other *pegasei*) takes the sarcophagus of Arlenari through the black hole Ae-Leiterra to the dimensional rift back on Earth; appears in *Win, Survive*.

Arlenari Kassiopei* (AHR-LEH-NAH-REE KAH-SEE-OH-PAY) – ancient Atlantean Imperial Kassiopei ancestor; daughter of "Blessed Churu" (Imperator) and Merneit Kassiopei, sister of Oron and Narmeradat, wife of Enhuvarat; calls herself "Arleana (AHR-LEH-AH-NAH), Starlight Sorceress," and is able to travel by means of Starlight; author of the diary called *The Book of Everything*; associates with an ancient someone named "Semmi;" designed the *astroctadra* windows in the Imperial Crown Prince and Imperial Princess's bedrooms; was officially erased from history; sealed inside a Pegasus Blood jewel within a sarcophagus discovered in the Yellow Habitat of Vimana on the surface of the Ghost Moon; is in stasis (not dead) and travels the Ship of Eternity; the Ghost Moon is later named after her; Gwen and Aeson's first child and eldest daughter is named after her; mentioned in *Survive*; appears in the prequel series ***Dawn of the Atlantis Grail***.

Asclep (AHSK-LEH-P) – Nomarch of Septu Station; killed in the destruction of Septu Station by the golden light spheres of the alien grid, appears in *Survive*.

Ashley (Rosen) – Candidate assigned to Yellow Quadrant Dorm Eight at the Pennsylvania RQC-3; bullies Gwen; skinny blonde; appears in *Qualify*.

Asiwet* (AH-SEE-WEH-T), Lord – Member of the Imperial Executive Council (IEC); political position: tell the general public of Atlantis about the alien threat; mentioned in *Win*.

Auntie Janice* – Janice Aimes, Laronda Aimes's aunt and legal guardian back on Earth, stays behind with Laronda's little brother Jamil; mentioned in *Qualify, Compete, Survive*.

Australian Guy, aka "The Aussie Guy" – nameless Qualified Candidate on board Ark-Ship 1109, described as "a dark-haired teen with an Aussie accent;" appears in *Compete*; has only two sentences of dialogue but plenty of reader fans!

Avaneh Lehatut (AH-VAH-NEH LEH-HAH-TOOT) – Games Contender, Red Warrior Category; joins Team Lark in Blue Stage Two; fierce, pale golden tan skin, dark blue eyes, shaved head, tattoos, silent; hired assassin sent to kill Gwen; offers her life to Gwen in an honorable death when she cannot obey her orders to kill Gwen (because Gwen possesses Aeson's black armband); commits suicide by falling to her death to keep her honor; appears in *Win*.

Axela Buiri (AH-KSEH-LAH BOO-EE-REE) – SPC Pilot assigned (along with Xurut Ralafi) as crew to Gwen and Oalla's *khepri* on the first *astroctadra* mission, their team headed to Mar-Yan; young, tall, brown-skinned woman, black hair, startling green eyes; appears in *Survive*.

B

Babi (BAH-BEE) – call sign of unspecified SPC Pilot at Tammuz during a space battle with the alien golden light grid; appears in *Survive*.

Bakar Ramajet (BAH-KAHR RAH-MAH-JET) – Hetmet (ruler) of Khenneb; requests Gwen's help with a difficult *pegasei* retrieval from an illegal subterranean facility hidden inside mountain caves in the nation of Khenneb; supports the PRT mission; appears in *Survive*.

Baritei "Bari" Gaido (BAH-REE-TAY GUY-DOH) – Fleet crewman on ICS-2; aligned with the Blue Quadrant; dances with Gracie at the Blue Zero-G Dance until Blayne arrives; appears in *Compete*.

Bavaam Vekahat (BAH-VAH-AHM VEH-KAH-HAH-T), Lord – Xelio's father; bears an ancient familial grudge against the Kassiopei Dynasty; disturbed and addicted to substances; commits *im-seki*, leaving Xelio to be the young Lord of the House Vekahat; mentioned in *Aeson: Blue*.

Becca Marlin – Candidate assigned to Red Quadrant Dorm Five at the Pennsylvania RQC-3; friend of Gracie; disqualified at NQC for involvement with the shuttle sabotage incident at RQC-3; appears in *Qualify*.

Bequa Larei (BEH-KWAH LAH-RAY) – Captain of Ark-Ship 1109 (AS-1109), Gwen's original ark-ship; transfers Gwen to ICS-2 on Decision Day, after Gwen announces her life choice of "Citizen;" appears in *Compete*.

Bevi (BEH-VEE) – custodian and cleaning woman in Fleet Cadet School dormitory; teaches young Aeson janitorial duties; appears in *Aeson: Blue*.

Bill Anderson – Eastern National Network (ENN) prime time news anchor; one of many media personalities around the globe who present the Qualification Semi-Finals on Earth; works with co-anchor Cathy Estrada; appears in *Qualify*.

Blair – Candidate who occupies bunk next to Gwen at the NQC; member of Team USA 14 during Qualification Finals, letter assignment unknown; appears in *Qualify*.

Blayne Dubois – see Major Characters.

Brie Walton – see Gabriella; see Major Characters.

Buhaat Hippeis (BOO-HAH-AT HEE-PEH-EES) – Atlantean media personality; Host of *Winning the Grail*, a popular sports and entertainment show dedicated to the Games that interviews Contenders and covers the Games of the Atlantis Grail; Tiago's media rival; thin and wiry, with enthusiastic tenor voice; appears in *Win, Survive*.

C

Carilla Oruvi (KAH-REEL-lah OH-ROO-vee) – Lady of House Oruvi; 11th generation, Low Court; from Eastern Vadat Province; introduced to Gwen at the Ladies of the Court Bridal event; appears in *Survive*.
Carlos Villa – Section Leader of Yellow Quadrant Section Fourteen / Team 14 at the NQC; appears in *Qualify*.
Carrie Willis – student at Mapleroad Jackson High School; Gwen's classmate; has an ugly purple-and-orange travel bag; appears in *Qualify*.
Cathy Estrada – Eastern National Network (ENN) prime time news anchor; one of many media personalities around the globe who present the Qualification Semi-Finals on Earth; works with co-anchor Bill Anderson; appears in *Qualify*.
Charles Lark – see Major Characters.
Charlie Venice – Candidate assigned to Red Quadrant Dorm Five at the Pennsylvania RQC-3; friend of Gracie; member of Team USA 14, letter assignment unknown; appears in *Qualify*.
Chiar Nuridat (CHEE-AHR NUH-REE-DAH-T) – Pilot First Rank; aligned with Red Quadrant; nineteen years old; seven years in the Fleet; killed in the shuttle sabotage incident at the Pennsylvania RQC-3; mentioned in *Qualify*; appears in *Aeson: Black*.
Chihar Agwath (CHEE-HAH-R AH-GWAH-TH) – Games Contender, Blue Scientist Category; joins Team Lark in Red Stage One and continues to remain on Team Lark for the duration of The Games; hallucinates his deceased father berating him during Blue Stage Two; motive for entry in the Games: to purchase the majority seat on the Committee of Education of Tatenen in the Western Xeneret Province so that children can learn Science and the Arts properly; finalist in the Blue Scientist Category; loses tiebreaker event, but Gwen grants his wish through her own Champion Wish by naming him her permanent voting proxy on her primary seat on the Tatenen Committee of

Education; older man, red leathery skin, white hair, balding, careful, soft-spoken; appears in *Win, Survive*.

Chimaida (CHEE-MY-DAH) – Tiliar's Zero-G Dance date at Fleet Cadet School; appears in *Aeson: Blue*.

Chior Kla (CHEE-OHR KLAH) – Atlantean Language Instructor on ICS-2; Civilian; aligned with Yellow Quadrant; appears in *Compete*.

Chiyoko Sato – see Major Characters.

Chris – Candidate assigned to Yellow Quadrant Dorm Eight; tall, athletic boy in Agility class who easily swings on the monkey bars scaffolding; appears in *Qualify*.

Chris Jasper – student at Mapleroad Jackson High School; one of Gwen's bullies; appears in *Qualify*.

Chudo Batiaxaat (CHOO-DOH BAHT-YAH-KSAH-AHT) – SPC Command Pilot of War-3; crew primarily National Fleet from Ubasti; escorts Anen Qur to Septu during the final Helios system *astroctadra* mission; appears in *Survive*.

Churu Kassiopei* (CHOO-ROO KAH-SEE-OH-PAY) – ancient Imperator in power when Atlanteans escape Earth and settle on the colony planet; dies within a year of Landing on the planet Atlantis; referred to as "Blessed Churu;" father of Arlenari, Oron, and Narmeradat, husband to Merneit; mentioned in *Survive*; appears in the prequel series *Dawn of the Atlantis Grail*.

Claudia Grito – Candidate assigned to Yellow Quadrant Dorm Eight at the Pennsylvania RQC-3; ranks #942 going into the Semi-Finals; assigned to Team USA 14C in the Finals; bullies Gwen throughout Qualification; saved by Gwen during the subterranean tunnel race in the Finals; Qualifies; one of six *shìrén* Cadet Pilots assigned to Gwen's PRT on the *Pegasei* Retrieval Khenneb Mission; uses herself as human shield to protect Gwen during mission; Latina, curvy, sinewy muscle, raven-black hair in a long ponytail, sultry good looks; multiple piercings with smart jewelry, later removed to comply with Fleet regulations; appears in *Qualify, Survive*.

Conrad Hart – Qualified Candidate originally from South Africa; Cadet Pilot Partner of Alla Vetrova; ranks #1 at the beginning of the first Cadet QS Race; earns 100% and ranks #1 at the end of the first Cadet QS Race; ranks #1 at beginning of the second QS Race; earns 100% and ranks #1 (champion) at the end of the second QS Race; appears in *Compete*.

Consul Denu (DEH-NOO) – see Suval Denu; see Major Characters.

Corrector Arwai* (AHR-WAH-EE) – Corrector at the Poseidon Central Correctional Facility who works with Logan, supervising and handling Brie Walton; mentioned in *Win*.

Corwell* – see Quentin Corwell.

Craig Beller – Candidate assigned to Red Quadrant Dorm Five; martial artist who excels at karate, kickboxing, and Er-Du; ranks #4 at the Pennsylvania RQC-3, going into the Semi-Finals; sandy-blond, compact; appears in *Qualify*.

Cretheo (KREH-THEH-OH) – Nomarch of Tammuz Station; barely escapes with his life on an *ardukat* to War-8, after safely evacuating everyone from Tammuz Station which is destroyed by the golden light spheres of the alien grid; appears in *Survive*.

Culuar Efrebu (KOO-LOO-AHR EH-FREH-BOO) – *astra daimon* with striking pale grey eyes; is one of the *daimon* at Aeson's initiation ceremony; "gives his light" at the Wedding Ceremony; goes to rescue Manala and others marooned in space at the end of the final Helios system *astroctadra* mission; appears in *Survive, Aeson: Black*.

D

Danaat* (DAH-NAH-AHT) – Nomarch at Ishtar Station; mentioned in *Survive*.

Daniel Tover – Qualified Candidate assigned to Red Quadrant Dorm One at the Pennsylvania RQC-3; member of Team USA 14 in the Qualification Finals, letter assignment unknown; Logan's friend and Earth Union (EU) operations partner; assigned to Red Quadrant, Drive and Propulsion, Cadet Deck One Barracks on ICS-1; Agrees with Logan that EU has been corrupted and is willing to cooperate with Atlantis; appears in *Qualify*, mentioned in *Compete*.

Darius Harrod – one of six *shìrén* Cadet Pilots assigned to Gwen's final PRT unit on the *Pegasei* Retrieval Khenneb Mission; pro athlete swimmer, runner, and lifeguard from Australia; tall, brown haired, green eyes; appears in *Survive*.

Darumet Azai (DAH-ROO-MEH-T AH-ZAH-EE) – the First Priest of Amrevet-Ra, the "other" Venerable One; in charge of the Groom during the Wedding events and preparations; officiates the Wedding Ceremony together with the First Priestess of Amrevet-Ra, Therutat Nuudri; thin, slight man with sparse, undyed greying hair; appears in *Survive*.

Dawn Williams – see Major Characters.

DeeDee Kim – Qualified Candidate originally from the Philippines; Cadet Pilot Partner of Leopold Deller; one of top three Pilot and Co-Pilot Pairs; earns 97% Fleet Score and ranks #4 at the end of the second Cadet QS Race; appears in *Compete*.

Deneb Gratu (DEH-NEH-B GRAH-TOO) – Games Contender, Red Athlete Category; specialty: professional skyball player; most favored Celebrity Contender; kidnaps Gwen during Red Stage One, and keeps her for her Favorite Kill points value as part of his team; abandons Gwen when convenient and uses her as bait to lure other high-profile teams while he hides with the Red Grail; falls to his death from his *pegasus* in the aerial portion of the Triathlon Race in Yellow Stage Four; big, tall, river-red clay skin, cold blue eyes; hard, mean, ruthless, competitive; appears in *Win*, mentioned in *Survive*.

Derek Sunder – Candidate assigned to Yellow Quadrant Dorm Eight at the Pennsylvania RQC-3; assigned to Team USA 14C in Finals; alpha bully who engages in "hashtagging" Blayne Dubois; bullies Gwen, steals her Yellow Quadrant Weapon (green woven net) during Combat class, which prompts her to tie her shoelaces together and become Shoelace Girl; big, bulky, dark-haired, with serpent neck tattoo; appears in *Qualify*.

Desher Keigeri (DEH-SHEH-R KAY-GEH-REE) – chief commentator for the Helios-Ra Imperial Poseidon Network (HRIPN), the largest media conglomerate in Imperial *Atlantida*; Lord of House Keigeri, 292nd generation, High Court, but goes by *"Ter"* in his media work; Oalla's father; interviews Manakteon Resoi when Earth refugees arrive;

interviews Gwen and Aeson in a media event before the Wedding; anchors the news; handsome, middle-aged, shoulder-length gilded hair, soulful deep blue eyes; appears in *Win, Survive*.

Desiree Bell – Candidate who ranks #5 at the Pennsylvania RQC-3, going into the Semi-Finals; super-dark hair, dark brown skin; very quick, very strong; appears in *Qualify*.

Devora Kassiopei (DEH-VOR-ah KAH-SEE-OH-PAY) – see Major Characters.

Dionte Jones – Candidate assigned to Yellow Quadrant Dorm Eight at the Pennsylvania RQC-3; appears in *Qualify*.

Drone Master, The – see Oshaharat Feveh.

Duu Valam (DOO-OOH VAH-LAHM) – Rai (ruler) of Bastet; proud of Bastet's Niktos Fleet that serves on War-8; dark-haired, red clay skin, indeterminate age, sharp features, prominent nose; appears in *Survive*.

E

Eddie – student at Mapleroad Jackson High School; friend of George; appears in *Qualify*.

Ekit Jei (EH-KEET JEH-EE) – Pilot of shuttle (together with Pilot Radra Vilai) that takes the Candidates on Team USA 14C to the location of the Qualification Finals; compact and muscular, river-red-clay skin; appears in *Qualify*.

Elikara Vekahat (EH-LEE-KAH-rah VEH-KAH-HAH-T) – see Major Characters.

Emilio Flores – Candidate aligned with the Yellow Quadrant; assigned to Team USA 14C in the Qualification Finals; appears in *Qualify*.

Enhuvarat* (EN-HOO-VAH-RAH-T) – ancient Atlantean husband of Arlenari Kassiopei, his family name unknown; mentioned in Survive, appears in the prequel series ***Dawn of the Atlantis Grail***.

Eodea Tecpatl (EH-OH-DEH-AH TEK-PAH-T-L) – SPC Command Pilot on War-10 carrying a training crew of Cadet Pilots from Ankh-Tawi and Weret; killed in the attack on Rah Station which is destroyed by the golden light spheres of the alien grid; appears in *Survive*.

Erin Tsai – Qualified Candidate aligned with the Blue Quadrant; ranks #1 at the Pennsylvania RQC-3; member of Team USA 14 during Qualification Finals, letter assignment unknown; Qualifies; assigned to Blue Quadrant, Network Systems, Cadet Deck Two Barracks on ICS-2; ranks #2 at the beginning of the first QS Race; earns 99% and Ranks #2 at the end of the first QS Race; ranks #2 at the beginning of the second QS Race; earns 98% and Ranks #3 at the end of the second QS Race; Pilot paired with her brother Roy Tsai; tall, athletic, short blue-black spiked hair; appears in *Qualify, Compete*.

Erita Hasmik Kassiopei* (EH-REE-TAH HAH-SMEE-K KAH-SEE-OH-PAY) – fifth child and youngest (infant) daughter of Gwen and Aeson; Imperial Princess; mentioned in *Survive*, will appear in future books.

Erita Qwas (EH-REE-TAH KWAH-S) – see Major Characters.

Etamharat Kassiopei* (EH-TAHM-HAH-RAH-T KAH-SEE-OH-PAY) – former Imperator, father of Romhutat; Aeson's paternal grandfather; aligned with the Green Quadrant; tells Aeson stories of myth and antiquity in a *storyteller* voice; after the death of his wife Hesper, loses the will to live and abdicates his Imperial Throne; dies during a Rim Maintenance Mission trying to stop a cascade reaction when the Great Quantum Shield fails, by sacrificing himself to save the Fleet; earns black armband of Honor; instructs Romhutat to enact the Earth Mission to close the dimensional rift; mentioned in *Survive, Aeson: Blue*.

Ethan Jamerson – Candidate aligned with the Green Quadrant; joins Gwen's informal team during the Qualification Semi-Finals; attends Gwen's stealth birthday party at the NQC; lanky, tall and skinny like a beanpole, pale brown hair, slightly disjointed nose, sharp jawline; appears in *Qualify*.

Evandros (Ayan) (EH-VAHN-DROH-S, [AH-YAHN]) – Nomarch at Atlantis Station; acting SPC Commander in the Commander's absence; in charge of the SPC HQ; aligned with the Green Quadrant; known for training *astra daimon*; hosts the Green Zero-G Dance on board the Atlantis Station before the final mission and battle; middle-aged, with bronze leathery skin, wrinkle-lined face, dark greying hair, minimal gold dye; stern, fair, thorough, relentless; appears in *Survive, Aeson: Black*.

F

Fadut (FAH-DOOT) – Games Contender, White Entrepreneur Category; member of Team Gratu starting from Red Stage One; gaunt, dark-skinned; appears in *Win*.

Fahid (FAH-HEED) – student in Fleet Cadet School; stocky boy who partners to fight Aeson in Combat Class; defeated by Aeson who scores points over him and wins the sparring match; appears in *Aeson: Blue*.

Fawzi Boto (FAHW-ZEE BOH-TOH) – Games Contender, White Vocalist Category; specialty: famous tenor in the *Atlantida* opera; member of Team Irtiu; part of the Plural Voice chorus attack in Blue Stage Two; finalist (along with Sofia Veforoi) and Gwen's rival in the Games Vocalist Category tiebreaker; unsuccessfully contests Gwen's win; his wish to purchase the Yatet Opera House and opera company in Poseidon granted by Gwen via her own Champion Wish; large, gilded hair, river-red-clay skin; appears in *Win, Survive*.

Felekamen Gori (FEH-LEH-KAH-MEHN GOH-REE) – Pilot Second Rank; aligned with the Yellow Quadrant; sixteen years old; five years in the Fleet; killed in the shuttle sabotage incident at the Pennsylvania RQC-3; mentioned in *Qualify*; appears in *Aeson: Black*.

Fuorai (FOO-OH-RAH-EE) – Lord of House Fuorai; Lady Tiri's father, First Lady Vahiz's husband; has a favorable arrangement with the Imperator that will go through if his daughter Tiri is chosen by Aeson as the Imperial Bride; proud, handsome, heavyset older man; appears in *Win, Survive*.

Futo (FUH-TOH) – a male comedian guest during intermission between Pre-Games Trials for the Games of the Atlantis Grail; does a comedy routine mocking sleepy Earth refugees, while speaking with Maga, a media commentator; has thick, dark eyebrows that he wiggles for comedic effect; appears in *Win*.

G

Gabriella "Brie" Walton – see Major Characters.

Gary Abbott – student assigned to room 115-B for the second portion of the Preliminary Qualification test at Mapleroad Jackson High School; appears in *Qualify*.

Gavreel (GAHV-REEL) – guard at Poseidon Central Correctional Facility (PCCF); former convict and reformed criminal; one of the experts Anu recruits to help train Gwen for the Games; teaches Gwen the hand piercing trick and (together with Krui) that "image is everything" for survival in the Games; tall, muscular brute with pale skin covered in tattoos, dull blue eyes; dense-looking but actually sharp and intelligent; appears in *Win*.

Gebi Girls, The – an all-girl music group formed after arrival on Atlantis; consists of four or five Earthies who play their own instruments, sing pop covers of old Earth and Atlantean music, and their own original material; appears in *Survive*.

Gennio Rukkat (GEH-NEE-OH ROOK-KAH-T) – see Major Characters.

George Lark – see Major Characters.

Ghara Vekahat (GHA-RAH VEH-KAH-HAH-T) – Elikara's mother, Xelio's aunt; Lady; widow of the House Vekahat and daughter of House Deksu that ends without progeny at 90th generation, High Court, and is absorbed into House Vekahat; introduced to Gwen at the Ladies of the Court Bridal event; beautiful, fragile, grieving; appears in *Survive*, *Aeson: Blue*.

Ghatak* – United Industan President; is aware (together with many other Earth leaders in the United Nations) of the stealth ark-ship AS-1999 in orbit around Earth; mentioned in *Survive*.

Gina Curtis – Candidate and Dorm Leader (DL) of Yellow Quadrant Dorm Eight at the Pennsylvania RQC-3; Section Fourteen Leader, Yellow Quadrant Dorm, USA Team 14 at the NQC; willowy African American girl with braided hair; appears in *Qualify*.

Gobu (GOH-BOO) – Member of the Imperial Executive Council (IEC); political position: Increase and improve monitoring surveillance for aliens; mentioned in *Win*.

Golden Mask – see "Rim, The"

Gordon "Gordie" Lark – see Major Characters.

Grace "Gracie" Lark – see Major Characters.

Greg Chee – Candidate assigned to Red Quadrant Dorm Five at the Pennsylvania RQC-3; friend of Gracie; member of Team USA 14 during Qualification Finals, letter assignment unknown; passes on news and gossip, brings up *Phoebos*; Chinese American with spiked black hair; appears in *Qualify*.

Gudun Yator (GOO-DOON YAH-TOHR) – Lady of House Yator, 16th generation, Low Court; introduced to Gwen at the Ladies of the Court Bridal event; friendly teen girl; appears in *Survive*.

Gwenevere "Gwen" Lark – see Major Characters.

H

Hasmik Tigranian - see Major Characters.

Hathora Sekru (HAH-THOH-rah SEH-kroo) – Lady of House Sekru; 74th generation, High Court; considered smart; part of Lady Tiri's posse at the Imperial Palace gardens; approves of Gwen dismissing Lady Tiri at the Ladies of the Court Bridal event; tall and stately, with tight gilded curls, fierce and heavy dark brows, dark eyes, bronzed skin; appears in *Win, Survive*.

Hedj Kukkait (HEHD-J KOOK-KAH-eet) – Games Contender, Red Warrior Category; known as "The White Bird;" called "Kuk-Ku!" by the public; popular Celebrity Contender; rescues Gwen from Deneb Gratu's Team during Red Stage One; Gwen pulls him out of the poisoned Safe Base to save him at the end of Red Stage One; rescues Gwen after she is shot in Green Stage Three; secretly works with Aeson's "The Rim" project to protect Gwen in the Games; Games Champion #2, Red Warrior Category, with 46,291 AG Points; Champion Wishes: open a major hospital complex in the Northern Mithektet Province to benefit the underserved agricultural population; organized labor leader, an *ertarat* (spiritual advisor, military discipline monk, nondenominational cleric, and medical professional); tall, gaunt, skeletal, intelligent face, pale skin, long white hair, black brows, strangely "avian" super-black eyes, hawk-like; appears in *Win, Survive*.

Hesper Kassiopei* (HEHS-PEHR KAH-SEE-OH-PAY) – former Imperatris; mother of Romhutat; Aeson's paternal grandmother; dies in a tragic accident a few years before her husband Etamharat, causing him to lose the will to live, and to abdicate his Imperial Throne; mentioned in *Survive, Aeson: Blue*.

Hijep Tiofon (HEE-JEHP TEE-OH-FOHN) – Atlantis Central Agency (ACA) Director; IEC Member; political position: keep everything secret from the public, return to Earth to pick up more people and resources before the asteroid hits, consider Earth UN an ally; Imperial loyalist and crony, impeccable courtier, part of the inner circle; middle aged, shoulder-length gilded hair, deep bronze skin, self-important demeanor; mentioned in *Win*, appears in *Survive*.

Hirat Sumbui* (HEE-RAHT SOOM-BOO-EE) – Captain of AS-1999, the ark-ship that stays behind on the Earth Mission and is orbiting Earth in stealth mode; Charles Lark, George Lark, and Margot Lark's remains are rescued and brought on board this ship; one of its four velo-cruisers is used by Quoni Enutat to bring the Larks to Atlantis; mentioned in *Survive*.

Horus – Trans-dimensional entity; golden being of pure light; takes on humanoid form with many arms to communicate with humans; ancient enemy of Atlantis; terminates the destructive OSIRIS program and grants peace to humanity when Gwen demonstrates the ability to use Starlight; appears in *Survive*.

Hugo Moreno – Qualified Candidate assigned to Blue Quadrant, Network Systems, Cadet Deck Two Barracks on ICS-2; Gwen's first Cadet Pilot Partner; ranks #547 at the beginning of the first Quantum Stream Race; earns 23% and ranks #624 (last place for their ark-ship) in the first race, after Breaching out of the Quantum Stream and ending up in interstellar space with Gwen; switches to a new Pilot Partner, Marc Goldstein; ranks #463 at the beginning of the second QS Race; earns 61% and ranks #419 at end of the second QS Race;

possibly Latin American, serious, dark-haired, speaks English with an accent, rude and dismissive of Gwen; appears in *Compete*.

I

Iela Nastasen* (EE-EH-lah NAH-stah-SEHN) – Lady of the House Nastasen; IEC member; political position: in favor of evacuation of Atlantis and founding a brand-new colony on another planet; mentioned in *Win*.

Igara Cvitu (EE-GAH-rah KVEE-too) – Imperial Poseidon Museum Antiquities Specialist; Original Colony Period expert; called upon to explore the lower levels of the buried ancient ark-ship Vimana, handle artifacts, read and translate Classical *Atlanteo*; dispatched to the Ghost Moon along with the others to analyze and handle the sarcophagus of Arlenari Kassiopei; dark-haired, middle-aged woman; appears in *Survive*.

Inevar Arelik (EE-NEH-VAHR AH-REH-LEEK) – Rai (ruler) of Ptahleon; complains of flooding in his country due to Ghost Moon tidal events; along with other heads of state, questions the feasibility of *pegasei* liberation with Arion; older man with parchment-pale light skin; composed, intelligent, dignified; appears in *Survive*.

Irana Nokut (EE-RAH-nah NOH-koot) – Lady of House Nokut; 55th generation, High Court; part of Lady Tiri's posse at the Imperial Palace gardens; owns a young pet *pegasus*; carries around Lady Tiri's drink until Gwen dismisses Tiri, then offers to get Gwen her own drink; approves of Gwen dismissing Lady Tiri at the Ladies of the Court Bridal event; at the Wedding, Gwen orders Lady Tiri to apologize to Lady Irana (and others); releases her pet *pegasus* after learning to communicate with it and realizing it is a sentient alien being; pretty and slender, porcelain-pale skin, stylish short straight hair; appears in *Win, Survive*.

Irumala Argosaen (EE-ROO-MAH-lah AHR-GOH-SAH-ehn) – First Lady of House Argosaen; wife of Lord Tutanamat Argosaen; mother of Devora; Aeson's maternal grandmother; introduced to Gwen at the Wedding; pleasant, elderly, with graceful features, greying dark brown hair, mischievous and charming smile; appears in *Survive*.

Isulat (EE-SOOH-LAHT) – Lady; priestess of Amrevet-Ra; assistant to the Venerable Therutat Nuudri; handles various Bridal details pertaining to the Wedding; slender, pretty, dark olive skin, gilded hair in a bun; gentle smile; appears in *Survive*.

Isabella Saltwater – Candidate aligned with the Red Quadrant; ranks #9 at the Pennsylvania RQC-3, going into the Semi-Finals; petite, with waist-long red hair, brilliant smile flashing white teeth; flirtatious; appears in *Qualify*.

Ishtar Sitamun* (EESH-TAHR SEE-TAH-MOON) – Lady of House Sitamun; IEC member; political position: tell the Earth refugees about the alien threat and keep it secret from the public; mentioned in *Win*.

Isis – Trans-dimensional entity; golden being of pure light; takes on humanoid form with many arms to communicate with humans; ancient enemy of Atlantis; terminates the destructive OSIRIS program and grants peace to humanity when Gwen demonstrates the ability to use Starlight; appears in *Survive*.

Iskandrat Suriner (EES-KAHN-DRAH-T SOO-REE-NEHR) – Lady of House Suriner; 38th generation, Middle Court; introduced to Gwen at the Ladies of the Court Bridal event; appears in *Survive*.

J

Jack – Candidate aligned with the Blue Quadrant; assigned to Team USA 14C at the NQC in Qualification Finals; appears in *Qualify*.

Jack Carell – Candidate assigned to Yellow Quadrant Dorm Eight at the Pennsylvania RQC-3; often runs in last place during Agility class; large, heavy, with curly blond hair; appears in *Qualify*.

Jaideep "Jai" Bhagat – Candidate assigned to Yellow Quadrant Dorm Eight at the Pennsylvania RQC-3; assigned to Team USA 14D at the NQC in Qualification Finals; Indian in appearance; bright, overly friendly smile that makes Gwen needlessly think he's hiding an evil side; loves to joke; appears in *Qualify*.

Jaime Robles – Candidate who ranks #7 at the Pennsylvania RQC-3, going into the Semi-Finals; stocky and tattooed; appears in *Qualify*.

Jake Dubois* – Blayne Dubois's younger brother, does not pass Preliminary Qualification; is good at many things, wants to change the world; mentioned in *Qualify*.

Jamil Aimes* – Laronda Aimes's six-year-old brother, too young for Qualification; mother, a single parent, died when Laronda was twelve, and Laronda and Jamil live with their guardian aunt; loves pizza; mentioned in *Qualify, Compete, Survive*.

Janice Aimes* – see Auntie Janice.

Janice Quinn – Candidate assigned to Yellow Quadrant Dorm Eight at the Pennsylvania RQC-3; sprains ankle; often rivals Gwen for last place in Agility class; pale and slight, with mousy-brown hair in a ponytail; appears in *Qualify*.

Jared Holder – Candidate from Venice Beach; aligned with the Red Quadrant; on Gwen's team at the Qualification Semi-Finals in Los Angeles; dives into the baton-filled pool to save Gracie; present at Gwen's secret birthday party at the NQC in Colorado; skinny older boy with a tan, weather-beaten, sandy blond longish hair; looks like a California surfer; light tenor voice; appears in *Qualify*.

Jeff Sangre* – Logan Sangre's older brother; twenty-two, too old for Qualification; in the military, deployed on his first tour of duty; Earth Union operative, recruits Logan for the EU; wants to die serving his country, not a senseless death by asteroid; gives Logan a knife which Logan gives to Gwen; mentioned in *Qualify*, will appear in future books.

Jennica Tulls – Qualified Candidate transferred (on the same shuttle with Gwen) from Ark-Ship 1109 to ICS-2; assigned to Red Quadrant, Residential Deck One; very tall, very dark-skinned, African American or African; appears in *Compete*.

Jenny – Qualified Candidate on ICS-2; member of Terra Patria; serves as lookout for Trey Smith in the Cadet Deck Four Meal Hall during hostage incident; told to disarm Aeson; killed by Aeson while outside the hall; appears in *Compete*.

Jenny Hawls – student at Mapleroad Jackson High School; bully Mark Gardner's girlfriend; bullies Gwen; bitchy and popular, model-perfect pretty face, long honey-blond hair; not too bright; appears in *Qualify*.

Jeremy Carverson – student at Mapleroad Jackson High School; bullies Gwen; appears in *Qualify*.

Jessica Conlett – Candidate assigned to Yellow Quadrant Dorm Eight at the Pennsylvania RQC-3; very young middle-schooler; unfamiliar with musical notes; appears in *Qualify*.

Jimmy Wong – Candidate who ranks #4 at New York RQC-1; shown on TV during the Semi-Finals media broadcast; appears in *Qualify*.

Joanie Katz* – student at Mapleroad Jackson High School; Logan's latest former girlfriend with whom he recently broke up; mentioned in *Qualify*.

John Nicolard – Candidate and Dorm Leader (DL) of Yellow Quadrant Dorm Eight at the Pennsylvania RQC-3; does not pass Semi-Finals; medium height, light brown hair, nondescript regular features; appears in *Qualify*.

Josh Merrow* – student at Mapleroad Jackson High School; friend of Logan; lead singer of their band (in which Logan plays lead guitar); mentioned in *Qualify*.

Joshua Bell – Candidate assigned to Yellow Quadrant Dorm Eight at the Pennsylvania RQC-3; good at martial arts; paired up with Gwen for Er-Du in Combat class; small, wiry middle-schooler or freshman from Philadelphia; energetic; appears in *Qualify*.

K

Kadeem Cantrell – Candidate assigned to Red Quadrant Dorm Nine; ranks #3 at the Pennsylvania RQC-3, going into the Semi-Finals; urban freerunner, parkour expert; runs on foot through streets of L.A. during Qualification Semi-Finals; Qualifies; assigned to Red Quadrant, Drive and Propulsion, Cadet Deck One Barracks on ICS-2; partnered with a French girl in Gwen's Pilot training class; fluent in French; very tall, skinny African American; appears in *Qualify, Compete*.

Kateb Nuletat (KAH-TEH-B NOO-LEH-TAH-T) – Games Contender, Yellow Inventor Category; with Team Gratu during Red Stage One; has a unique, long, folded trident weapon that unfurls into a bladed helicopter; volunteers to be responsible for Gwen when Team Gratu goes out to fight; works with Gwen and Vidam to use the water-filled drinking grails to create sound and disable the drone army; joins Team Lark in Blue Stage Two; motive for entry in the Games: to patent a device he invented to help his wife; tells Gwen and Brie a fable called "The Invention" when they are walled in by the pyramid stones; Games Champion #3, Yellow Inventor Category, with 6,137 AG Points; Champion Wishes: patent and manufacture a neural prosthetic device to help his wife and others to replicate musical tones, purchase a new house near Phoinios Heights; bland-looking young man with gilded hair in a segmented ponytail, hazel-green eyes; appears in *Win, Survive*.

Katherine Donahue – President of the United States; corrupt, together with many other Earth leaders in the United Nations; makes shady underhanded deals with Atlanteans; is aware of the stealth ark-ship AS-1999 in orbit around Earth; is aware and shows no concern that most of the Earth population cannot be saved due to age-based restrictions; issues order via Earth Union operatives to proceed with the hostage taking of Atlantean High Command operation to ensure her own and other select government heads' survival; appears in *Qualify*, mentioned in *Compete, Survive*.

Kem (KEH-M) – young assistant and personal aide to Consul Denu; does Gwen's hair and Face Art (overall design, hair detail arrangements, products selection, and cosmetics) and Face Paints (cosmetics color use) for the Red and Yellow Zero-G Dances; falls ill to Jump Sickness before the Quantum Jump, causing Gwen to help him get to his cabin (as a result, Gwen ends up with Aeson in the CP's cabin); does Gwen's hair and Face Art for Imperial Court functions; slim, dark-haired boy a little older than Gracie; appears in *Compete, Win, Survive*.

Ken Fisher – Candidate assigned to Yellow Quadrant Dorm Eight who ranks #6 at the Pennsylvania RQC-3, going into the Semi-Finals; smart, dark-haired boy Gwen's age with a street-tough stare; appears in *Qualify*.

Kephasa Sewu (KEH-FAH-SAH SEH-WOO) – the Oratorat (elected ruler) of Eos-Heket; on a state visit to Imperial *Atlantida*; introduced to

Gwen at an Imperial *dea* meal; impressed that Aeson and Gwen have a love match, not an arranged marriage; VIP guest invited to attend the Imperial Wedding; along with other heads of state, discusses the feasibility of *pegasei* liberation with Arion; bony, middle-aged woman with fair skin and handsome hawkish features, an aquiline nose, very dark eyebrows over deep-set eyes, dark brown hair in a stern knot; appears in *Survive*.

Keruvat Ruo (KEH-RUH-VAH-T ROO-OH) – see Major Characters.

Khadram Eetatu (KHAH-DRAH-M EE-EE-TAH-TOO) – Games Contender, Red Warrior Category; Lolu Eetatu's brother; offered in trade for Gwen by Team Gratu, which causes Lolu to betray Gwen; killed by Deneb Gratu before he can reach his sister in the Safe Base; young and thin teenage boy; appears in *Win*, mentioned in *Survive*.

Khemji (KEHM-JEE) – Manala Kassiopei's pet cat; oversized, fat, black, short-hair male feline; frequently passes gas; is reluctantly walked (dragged) on a harness leash; escapes through open window and causes Manala days of anguish; found and returned to Manala by George Lark who gets severely scratched up in the process; one of the author's own, recently rescued feral cats, named in honor of the fictional feline (Khemji Nazarian also passes gas, and is adorable); appears in *Win*, *Survive*.

Klavit Xotoi (KLAH-VEET KSOH-TOY) – Technology and Systems Instructor on ICS-2, Aligned with Blue Quadrant; teaches classes using hoverboards on the Hydroponics H-Deck, Manufacturing Deck, and more; tall and big, short gilded hair, reddish-brown skin, soft, pleasant, rounded features; appears in *Compete*.

Kokayi Jeet (KOH-KAH-EE JEE-T) – Games Contender, Green Entertainer Category; specialty: acrobat and body contortionist, martial arts dancer; joins Team Lark in Red Stage One; gets stuck in Lolu's poisoned web until she frees him; to save Gwen and revenge Zaap, shoots and kills Thalassa in the Triathlon Race in Yellow Stage Four; Games Champion #1, Green Entertainer Category, Green Stage Grail Winner; 60,479 AG Points (mostly inherited from Tiamat "Thalassa" Irtiu); Champion Wishes: Parade through Sky Tangle

City, purchase and renovate land and buildings for his own *orahemaeon*, improve the most rundown sections of Sky Tangle City; his father died in the Games some years earlier, so his *mamai* is not happy about Kokayi entering the Games also; tall, willowy, golden-brown skin, beautifully androgynous face, arched dark brows, three multi-colored braids; melodious voice; talkative; appears in *Win, Survive*.

Krui (KROO-EE) – guard at Poseidon Central Correctional Facility (PCCF); former convict and reformed criminal; former murderer and assassin, illiterate; one of the experts Anu recruits to help train Gwen for the Games; teaches Gwen the hand piercing trick and (together with Gavreel) that "image is everything" for survival in the Games; very short and compact, vaguely Earth-Asian looking, golden tan skin, leathery face, extremely defined muscles, messy short black hair, thick dark brows, dark eyes, low voice, thick accent in English; disturbing and creepy; appears in *Win*.

Kuz Ruo (KOO-Z ROO-OH) – First Lady of House Ruo; 97th generation, High Court, Keruvat's mother; introduced to Gwen at the Ladies of the Court Bridal event; very tall, willowy slim, short gilded hair, super dark skin; striking, warm, gracious, with a joyful smile; appears in *Survive*.

L

Lafaoh Ungreb (LAH-FAH-OH OON-GREH-B) – SPC Command Pilot on War-8; crew primarily Niktos Fleet from Bastet; safely escapes with all personnel evacuated from Tammuz Station just before it is destroyed by the golden light spheres of the alien grid; escorts Gordie to Tammuz in the Helios system second *astroctadra* mission; appears in *Survive*.

Larahat Sei (LAH-RAH-HAH-T SEH-EE) – Games Contender, Yellow Inventor Category; has a net of metallic fish-scale armor; tries to poison Gwen on day one of Red Stage One after falsely declaring a truce; possible assassin sent by the Imperator to eliminate Gwen; killed by Brie Walton; lean, of middle height, youngish, short wavy gilded hair; nervous-looking; appears in *Win*.

Laronda Aimes – see Major Characters.

Lars Hansen – Qualified Candidate transferred (on the same shuttle with Gwen) from Ark-Ship 1109 to ICS-2; assigned to Green Quadrant, Brake and Shields, Cadet Deck Three Barracks on ICS-2; older teen, very tall (over 6'4"), pale Scandinavian, shoulder-length flax-blond hair in a ponytail; haughty, tight-lipped expression; deep, soft, arrogant voice; appears in *Compete*.

Laurie Dubois* – Blayne Dubois's older sister; does not pass Preliminary Qualification; dreams of going to medical school, wants to be a doctor and save people; mentioned in *Qualify*.

Laz (LAH-z) – student in Fleet Cadet School; tall boy who partners to fight Aeson in Combat Class; defeated by Aeson who scores points over him and wins the sparring match; appears in *Aeson: Blue*.

Leetana Chipuo (LEE-EE-TAH-nah CHEE-POO-oh) – Games Contender, Green Animal Handler Category; Contender who first successfully harnesses a *pegasus* in Yellow Stage Four; Games Champion #4, Animal Handler Category; 5,804 AG Points; Champion Wishes: pardon for her incarcerated father; major renovations and clean water for her family's small town in the Western Xeneret Province; tall, long red-and-gold-streaked hair; confident, arrogant; appears in *Win, Survive*.

Leon Madongo – Qualified Candidate originally from Kenya, on board ICS-2; Blayne Dubois's Cadet Pilot Partner; ranks #351 at the beginning of the first Quantum Stream Race; earns 83% at the end of the first QS Race; ranks #173 at the beginning of the second QS Race; earns 93% and ranks #18 at the end of the second QS Race; brown skin, wiry; soft-spoken, mellow, friendly; appears in *Compete*.

Leopold Deller – Qualified Candidate originally from Austria, on board ICS-2; Cadet Pilot Partner of DeeDee Kim; one of top three Pilot and Co-Pilot Pairs; earns 97% Fleet Score and ranks #4 at end of the second Cadet QS Race; appears in *Compete*.

Li Jie – one of six *shìrén* Cadet Pilots assigned to Gwen's final PRT unit on the *Pegasei* Retrieval Khenneb Mission; muscular Chinese boy with shoulder-length black hair gathered in a segmented tail; reserved, not talkative; appears in *Survive*.

Ligerat Faroi (LEE-GEH-RAH-T FAH-RO-EE) – Atlantean representative who administers the hoverboard test at the Mapleroad Jackson High School auditorium during Preliminary Qualification; slim and tall man with gilded hair, deeply bronzed skin, prominent dark eyebrows, dark eyes, reminiscent of Ancient Egypt; appears in *Qualify*.

Lirama Rikat (LEE-RAH-MAH REE-KAH-T) – Pilot (together with Pilot Mikelion Wasi) of shuttle that takes the Candidates to Los Angeles for the Qualification Semi-Finals; *astra daimon*; gilded hair, beautiful and confident, deep tan, muscular build; appears in *Qualify*.

Liu Kao Wong* – Chinese President; is aware (together with many other Earth leaders in the United Nations) of the stealth ark-ship AS-1999 in orbit around Earth; mentioned in *Survive*.

Logan Sangre – see Major Characters.

Lolu Eetatu (LOH-LOO EE-EE-TAH-TOO) – Games Contender, Blue Technician Category; joins Team Lark during Red Stage One; enters the Games with her brother Khadram to help their dying mother receive medical care; betrays Team Lark by surrendering Gwen to Team Gratu in exchange for her brother (who gets killed anyway); in Blue Stage Two, cautiously accepted back on Team Lark by Gwen who feels sorry for her; saved by Gwen on the spinning pyramid at the end of Blue Stage Two; finalist in the Blue Technician Category; loses tiebreaker to Mineb Inei; becomes Gwen's Personal Assistant to repay Gwen for ensuring that Lolu's mother receives medical treatment (which fulfills Lolu's wish); petite, wiry, quick young girl (Gracie's age), short pixie-hair with streaks in four colors, intense eyes; young soprano voice; frequently annoyed; appears in *Win, Survive*.

M

Maga (MAH-GAH) – Games of the Atlantis Grail Pre-Games Trials commentator; talks with Futo, a comedian guest during intermission, as he does a comedy routine mocking sleepy Earth refugees; appears in *Win*.

Mamai-**Jeet** (MAH-MAH-EE JEE-T) – Kokayi's mother; disapproves of him participating in the Games because Kokayi's father died in the

Games and she is afraid of losing her son also; initially doesn't want to see Kokayi and his fellow Games Champions at her home during his Parade in Sky Tangle City, then relents and offers soup to all of them; skeletal-thin "hag," tall, middle-aged, brown skin, sunken face, large black eyes; mentioned in *Win*, appears in *Survive*.

Mamraj Shahad – Candidate who ranks #10 at the Pennsylvania RQC-3, going into the Semi-Finals; very dark, tall, intellectually brilliant; appears in *Qualify*.

Man in the golden mask – see "Rim, The."

Manakteon Resoi (MAH-NAHK-teh-ohn REH-SOH-ee) – Commander of the Atlantis Earth Mission Fleet and Aeson's commanding officer; Imperial Fleet Commander; aligned with the Green Quadrant; stationed on Imperial Command Ship One (ICS-1); Command Pilot in the Star Pilot Corps (SPC) assigned to War-1 and reporting to the SPC Commander Aeson Kassiopei; fixed, handsome face, gilded hair, black eyebrows; soft, rich, musical voice with leashed power; strange, lilting accent in English; appears in all novels and *Aeson: Black*.

Manala Kassiopei (MAH-NAH-lah KAH-SEE-oh-PAY) – see Major Characters.

Mara Vahad* (MAH-rah VAH-HAH-D) – Tiliar Vahad's older sister; Aeson calls her to notify the family about Tiliar's death; mentioned in *Aeson: Black*.

Marc Goldstein – Hugo Moreno's chosen second Cadet Pilot Partner; ranks #463 at the beginning of the second QS Race; earns 61% and ranks #419 at the end of the second QS Race; appears in *Compete*.

Margot Arlenari Kassiopei* (MAHR-goh AHR-leh-NAH-ree KAH-SEE-oh-PAY) – eldest daughter of Gwen and Aeson; Imperial Crown Princess and Heir to the Throne of Imperial *Atlantida*; five Atlantean years old; mentioned in *Survive*, will appear in future books.

Margot Lark – see Major Characters.

Mark Foster – Candidate and Dorm Leader (DL) of Yellow Quadrant Dorm Eight at the Pennsylvania RQC-3; Section Fourteen

Leader, Yellow Quadrant Dorm, USA Team 14 at the NQC; confident and authoritative; powerful, commanding voice; appears in *Qualify*.

Mark Gardner – student at Mapleroad Jackson High School; bullies Gwen; boyfriend of Jenny Hawls; big, burly, good-looking, popular, obnoxious; appears in *Qualify*.

Marksen – see Principal Marksen.

Mateo Perez – Candidate assigned to Yellow Quadrant Dorm Eight at the Pennsylvania RQC-3; assigned to Team USA 14C at the NQC in Qualification Finals; attends Gwen's secret birthday party at the NQC; Latino, stocky, olive skinned, with dark wavy hair; younger, possibly freshman, grim and serious; appears in *Qualify*.

Mayavat Meropei (MAH-YAH-VAH-T MEH-ROH-PAY) – SPC Command Pilot of War-7; crew primarily Lower Fleet of Shuria; escorts Aeson to Ishtar in the Helios system second *astroctadra* mission; appears in *Survive*.

Merneit Kassiopei* (MEHR-NEH-EET KAH-SEE-OH-PAY) – ancient Imperatris from the time period when Atlanteans escaped Earth and settled on the new colony planet; wife of Churu and mother of Narmeradat, Arlenari, and Oron; mentioned in Survive, appears in the prequel series ***Dawn of the Atlantis Grail***.

Mia Weston – Candidate assigned to Red Quadrant Dorm Five at the Pennsylvania RQC-3; Team USA 14, letter assignment unknown, at the NQC; friend of Gracie; runs to tell Gwen when Gracie is detained and Disqualified; petite, pretty, brown-haired; appears in *Qualify*.

Mikelion Wasi (MEE-KEH-LEE-OHN WAH-SEE) – Pilot (together with Pilot Lirama Rikat) of shuttle that takes the Candidates to Los Angeles for the Qualification Semi-Finals; *astra daimon*; long, gilded hair; commanding manner; appears in *Qualify*.

Mindy Clarence – student at Mapleroad Jackson High School; junior, Gwen's classmate; first student to be called to sing the "ee" sound test; appears in *Qualify*.

Mindy Erikson – student at Mapleroad Jackson High School; walks by as Gwen and her siblings are saying goodbye to their father; has flaming red hair; appears in *Qualify*.

Mineb Inei (MEE-NEHB EE-NEH-EE) – Games Contender, Blue Technician Category; finalist in the Blue Technician Category; wins tiebreaker and defeats Lolu Eetatu; Games Champion #8; 3,605 AG Points; Champion Wishes: Citizenship for his wife and children; start a hybrid tech company for integrating Earth and Atlantean technology using his share of the Common Earnings Grail; large, heavy man with messy, undyed brown hair; appears in *Survive*.

Miramis Opu (MEE-RAH-MEES OH-POO) – current Priest of the Grail, an annual designation; a temporary honorific position given each year to a favored member of the various sects of the Atlantean clergy; leads the Invocation, the Final Ceremony and other ceremonies of the Games; administers the Citizenship Oath to the Champions; not a large man but has a "large presence;" mentioned (not by name) in *Win*, appears in *Survive*.

Mirin (MEE-REEN) – student in Fleet Cadet School; girl who dates Xelio; assists young Oalla and Elikara in the "re-re-xut" escapade during their Fleet Cadet School days; mentioned in *Win*, appears in *Aeson: Blue*.

Mithrat Okoi (MEE-THRAH-T OH-KOY) – Pilot Training Instructor on ICS-2, aligned with the Blue Quadrant; was Aeson's Pilot Instructor in Fleet Cadet School; average height, grim, weathered, leathery skin, gaunt face, dark hair, greying at the temples, residue of gold dye; does not bother to properly dye his hair; harsh and unforgiving but fair and real, quick to punish for transgressions; appears in *Compete, Survive, Aeson: Blue, Aeson: Black*.

Miwat (MEE-WAH-T) – Imperial Palace maidservant assigned to assist Gwen on the day of her landing on Atlantis with spa treatments for the Imperial Court Assembly; sweet-faced girl; appears in *Compete*.

Mr. Borster* – AP History teacher at Mapleroad Jackson High School; teaches George and Logan in the same class; mentioned in *Qualify*.

Mr. Warrenson – Atlantis Tech Instructor for Yellow Quadrant Dorm Eight at the Pennsylvania RQC-3; teaches the basics of Atlantean sound technology from an Earth scientist perspective; is present when Gwen does the shuttle levitation demo; middle-aged, balding; mild, abstracted expression; appears in *Qualify*.

Mrs. Bayard – Preliminary Qualification test administrator at Mapleroad Jackson High School; wears four-color Atlantean armband; tests Gwen on spatial ability via drawing, Quadrant determining barrage of visual images, choice of four Quadrant items (knife, pen, shield, map), and the singing "ee" sound test; appears in *Qualify*.

Mrs. Grayland – Gwen's homeroom teacher at Mapleroad Jackson High School; takes roll call, assigns students their classrooms for the next portion of the Preliminary Qualification test; passes out test booklets for the standardized test general knowledge portion; appears in *Qualify*.

Ms. Wayne – Preliminary Qualification test administrator at Mapleroad Jackson High School; wears four-color Atlantean armband; gives a brief "introduction to Atlantis and asteroid situation" speech; administers the first portion, the standardized general knowledge test, according to the ACA and federal government instructions; takes Gwen's finished test booklet; bland, homegrown-stocky; blank, authoritative expression; appears in *Qualify*.

Music Mage – disc jockey voice acting role; mysterious, "sexy siren" voice, specially amplified, used to announce changes in gravity during a zero gravity dance; see Vazara Hotat.

Muutat Bisfuri* (MOO-OO-TAH-T BEES-FOO-REE) – ancient Atlantean architect chosen as the builder on record for the primary Imperial Palace structure on the colony planet Atlantis, upon the orders of the Kassiopei Dynasty; mentioned in *Survive*, appears in the prequel series ***Dawn of the Atlantis Grail***.

N

Nancy Andrew – student assigned to room 25-C for the second portion of the Preliminary Qualification test at Mapleroad Jackson High School; appears in *Qualify*.

Narmeradat Kassiopei* (NAHR-MEHR-AH-DAH-T KAH-SEE-OH-PAY) – ancient Imperial Crown Prince and Heir, son of Churu Kassiopei;

becomes Imperator when Churu dies soon after Landing; mentioned in *Survive*, appears in the prequel series ***Dawn of the Atlantis Grail***.

Nefir Mekei (NEH-FEER MEH-KEH-EE) – see Major Characters.

Nepht (NEHF-T) – call sign of unspecified SPC Pilot at Tammuz, fighting the alien golden light grid formation; appears in *Survive*.

Nergal Duha (NEHR-GAHL DOO-HAH) – *astra daimon*; is present at Aeson's *astra daimon* initiation ceremony; "gives his light" at the Wedding Ceremony; asks Gordie to dance at the green Zero-G Dance; goes to rescue Manala and others marooned in space at the end of the final Helios system *astroctadra* mission; lean, tall, very dark skin; appears in *Survive, Aeson: Black*.

Nick Warren – student at Mapleroad Jackson High School; football jock and Gwen's classmate; walks by with his younger brother as Gwen and her siblings are saying goodbye to their father; appears in *Qualify*.

Nilara Gradat (NEE-LAH-RAH GRAH-DAHT) – Culture Instructor on ICS-2; aligned with the Yellow Quadrant; office #34 on Residential Deck Four; teacher at Lyceum School in Thetis Nereo, a coastal city in Imperial *Atlantida*; teaches the Earthies about Atlantean holidays, zero gravity dancing, social relations, and more; curvy, older teen, gilded hair in a knot, oval face, friendly brown eyes; appears in *Compete*.

O

Oalla Ann Kassiopei* (OH-AHL-LAH [ANN] KAH-SEE-OH-PAY) – second daughter and fourth child of Gwen and Aeson; Imperial Princess; two Atlantean years old; mentioned in *Survive*, will appear in future books.

Oalla Keigeri (OH-AHL-LAH KAY-GEH-REE) – see Major Characters.

Oliver Parker – Logan Sangre's Cadet Pilot Partner; ranks #7 at the beginning of the first Quantum Stream Race; earns 98% and ranks #3 at the end of the first QS Race; ranks #3 at the beginning of the second QS Race; earns 99% and ranks #2 at the end of the second QS Race; appears in *Compete*.

Olivia (Colway) – Candidate assigned to Yellow Quadrant Dorm Eight at the Pennsylvania RQC-3; Ranks #2,315 at RQC-3; alpha bully who engages in "hashtagging" Blayne Dubois; bullies Gwen; sleek, auburn-haired, curvy, well-endowed, older teen; Dawn Williams thinks she has a "nice rack;" appears in *Qualify*.

Oron Kassiopei* (OH-ROHN KAH-SEE-OH-PAY) – ancient Imperial Prince, twin brother of Arlenari; erased from history because he stayed on Earth; mentioned in *Survive*, appears in the prequel series ***Dawn of the Atlantis Grail***.

Oshaharat Feveh (OH-SHA-HAH-RAHT FEH-VEH) – Games Contender, Blue Technician Category; originally called "The Drone Master" by Brie Walton because of his invincible drone army; nickname picked up by everyone else; assumes the Favorite Kill points status from Gwen; falls to his death while climbing scaffolding, trying to reach the Safe Base occupied by Gwen, Kateb, and Vidam; his drones wreak general havoc until reprogrammed by Gwen and the others; his Favorite Kill points reassigned to Ujaste Naat; wiry, of average build, physically unremarkable; longish dark hair with faded gold streaks, careless dye job; sharp, clear tenor voice; appears in *Win*.

OSIRIS (OH-SEE-REE-TH) – ancient destructive program (automated cosmic sequence) set to destroy (cleanse) humanity on Atlantis and Earth; generates sphere objects (energy scattering machines powered by the local star) to cleanse within a specified diameter, with a solar engine at its center; old, brute-force program no longer in use, but left running over 10,000 years; recalled and deactivated by "Them," the golden trans-dimensional aliens, when Gwen demonstrates the ability to wield Starlight; appears in *Survive*.

Osuo Menbuut (OH-SUH-OH MEHN-BOO-OOT) – Rai (ruler) of Shuria; man of indeterminate years, very black hair, bronze skin; appears in *Survive*.

P

Peleset Frawei* (PEH-LEH-SET FRAH-WAY) – Arch Corrector in charge of the Legal and Correctional Agency (LCA) and all the law enforcement in Poseidon; mentioned in *The Atlantis Grail Companion*.

Pheret Aduo* (PHEH-REH-T AH-DOO-OH) – Aeson's very first Imperial Aide when he was young; accompanies Aeson in the shuttle to the fishing village Nifa to recruit Anu Vei; leaves his position in Aeson's employ due to family issues; replaced by Anu Vei; mentioned in *Win*.

Principal Marksen – Principal of Mapleroad Jackson High School; introduces Ligerat Faroi in the auditorium for the Preliminary Qualification hoverboard test; hands out encoded ID tokens to the students, administers the process and maintains order; appears in *Qualify*.

Q

Qedeh Adamer (KEH-DEH AH-DAH-MEHR) – Hetmet (ruler) of Qurartu; mourns the destruction of Septu Station, War-9, and the crew from Qurartu; appears in *Survive*.

Qeth Vekahat (KEH-TH VEH-KAH-HAH-T) – Elikara Vekahat's father; attends his daughter's Fleet Cadet School Graduation together with his wife, Ghara; dies together with Elikara while on a classified Imperial Fleet advance reconnaissance preliminary Earth Mission; appears in *Aeson: Blue*.

Quarar Ritazet* (KOO-AH-RAHR REE-TAH-ZEHT) – Command Pilot of Imperial Command Ship Four (ICS-4) in the Earth Mission Fleet, the rear anchor ship (end center) of the three-column Fleet formation; taken hostage on his ship during the Terra Patria takeover incident (incited by Earth Union operatives); aligned with the Yellow Quadrant; mentioned in *Compete*.

Quaratha* (KOO-AH-RAH-THAH) – elderly Dame at Lady Hathora's reception who tells "daft stories," as described by Lady Tiri; related to Lady Hathora's second cousin's brother-in-law; mentioned in *Aeson: Black*.

(Quentin) Corwell* – British Prime Minister; is aware (together with many other Earth leaders in the United Nations) of the stealth ark-ship AS-1999 in orbit around Earth; mentioned in *Survive*.

Quoni Enutat (KOO-OH-NEE EH-NUH-TAHT) – see Major Characters.

Qurume Ateni (KOO-ROO-MEH AH-TEH-NEE) – Aquatics Instructor at the NQC in Colorado, USA; teaches swimming; tall, willowy, with his gilded hair in a tight multi-segmented ponytail; has a wry and outrageously disdainful sense of humor; appears in *Qualify*.

R

Radanthet Ulumaq (RAH-DAHN-THEH-T OO-LOO-MAHK) – *astra daimon* from Shuria; assigned to War-7 and Ishtar Station; called "Radan" by Oalla; nicknamed "Rad-Rad" by Erita Qwas; brings Erita *fuchmik* (dessert) from Khur, Shuria; is present at Aeson's *astra daimon* initiation ceremony; "gives his light" at the Wedding Ceremony; dances with Erita at the Wedding; goes to rescue Manala and others marooned in space at the end of the final Helios system *astroctadra* mission; medium height, muscular and slightly heavyset, curling gilded hair, light bronze skin; mentioned in *Win*, appears in *Survive, Aeson: Black.*

Radra Vilai (RAH-DRAH VEE-LAH-EE) – Pilot of shuttle (together with Pilot Ekit Jei) that takes the Candidates on Team USA 14C to the location of the Qualification Finals; rich alto voice, gilded hair; appears in *Qualify*.

Rea Bunit (REH-AH BOO-NEET) – Games Contender, Blue Scientist Category; finalist in the Blue Scientist Category; wins tiebreaker against Chihar Agwath; Games Champion #10; 3,394 Total AG Points; Champion Wishes: admission to the prestigious STA Lyceum and Academy of High Technology at Poseidon as a high-level student (with security clearance), daughter will become Citizen (since both parents are now Citizens); petite, dark-skinned; appears in *Survive*.

Reporters (various) – members of the media asking questions during Bridal Media Event, from the following venues:

Free Poseidon News
News of the Golden Bay
The Daily Bay Flow
Talk and Laugh News Digest
Eos News Feed

Contemporary Court Style and Gossip
Bay City News and Entertainment

Rertu (REHR-TOO) – Nomarch of Rah Station; killed when the station and War-10 are destroyed by the golden light spheres of the alien grid; appears in *Survive*.

Rim, The – a mysterious golden mask against a black background; cuts in during various critical moments of the Games with anti-establishment propaganda; an illicit entity, member of a mysterious group entitled "The Rim," interrupts local media broadcasts, mostly the Games coverage; claims to support the Earth Bride; Aeson reveals to Gwen that he is the Rim, and that Anu and Gennio are in on it, together with Hedj Kukkait, in order to keep Gwen safe during the Games, appears in *Win*, mentioned in *Survive*.

Romhutat "Rommi" Charles Kassiopei (ROHM-HOO-TAH-T "ROHM-MEE" [CHARLES] KAH-SEE-OH-PAY) – first son and second child of Gwen and Aeson; Imperial Prince; twin brother of Suval Gordon; three and a half Atlantean years old; mentioned in *Survive*, will appear in future books.

Romhutat Kassiopei (ROHM-HOO-TAH-T KAH-SEE-OH-PAY) – see Major Characters.

Rovat Bennu (ROH-VAHT BEHN-NOO) – Science and Technology Agency (STA) Director; Imperial loyalist; IEC Member: political position: mobilize the Fleet, otherwise not particularly political, more interested in science; discovers correlation between ancient ark-ship signal and Ghost Moon appearance; long, leathery face, late middle-aged, sparse dark brown hair barely gilded around a large bald spot; mentioned in *Win*, appears in *Survive*.

Roy Tsai – Qualified Candidate aligned with the Blue Quadrant; ranks #2 at the Pennsylvania RQC-3; member of Team USA 14 during Qualification Finals, letter assignment unknown; Qualifies; assigned to Blue Quadrant, Network Systems, Cadet Deck Two Barracks on ICS-2; ranks #2 at the beginning of the first QS Race; earns 99% and ranks #2 at the end of the first QS Race; ranks #2 at the beginning of the second QS Race; earns 98% and ranks #3 at the end of the second QS Race; Pilot paired with his sister Erin Tsai; tall, athletic, short blue-black spiked hair; appears in *Qualify, Compete*.

Rumeiar Heru (ROO-MEH-YAR HEH-ROO) – *astra daimon*; aligned with the Blue Quadrant; inspires young Fleet Cadet School *kefarai* Aeson to strive to become *astra daimon*; present at Aeson's *astra daimon* initiation ceremony; part of the Deshi Royal House, fifth in line for the Deshi Throne; older, tall and lean, with a copper-red cast to his skin; appears in *Aeson: Blue, Aeson: Black*, will appear in future books.

Rurim Kiv (ROO-RIM KEE-V) – Games Contender, Yellow Artist Category; specialty: magician illusionist and entertainer; enters the Games as Artist because the Entertainer category has too many high-profile Contenders; retrieves the Blue Grail, becomes Winner of Blue Stage Two; Games Champion #5, Yellow Artist Category; 4,107 AG Points; Champion Wishes: that his performance art (as an illusionist) be admitted for display in the highest Poseidon cultural arts center, and granted eligibility for the full honors of his profession; member of group sent to investigate the ancient Vimana ark-ship; super-dark black skin, muscular, perfectly defined body, very handsome, tightly curling short gilded hair, brown eyes, graceful arched brows; confident, relaxed expression; appears in *Win, Survive*.

S

Saiva Neidos* (SAH-EE-VAH NEH-EE-DOHS) – SPC Command Pilot of War-4; crew primarily Republic Fleet from Eos-Heket; stationed near Olympos Station, remains in the outer system throughout the alien conflict; mentioned in *Survive*.

Samantha* – Lark family cat that badly scratched George when he was a seven-year-old, and he ended up going to the ER for antibiotics, on the insistence of his parents, just in case; mentioned in *Survive*.

Samuel Duarte – Candidate who ranks #8 at the Pennsylvania RQC-3, going into the Semi-Finals; aligned with the Green Quadrant; tall, burly, older teen, huge muscular arms, wide shoulders; sharp attitude; appears in *Qualify*.

Sarah Thornwald – Candidate from North Carolina (with a British father); aligned with the Green Quadrant; joins Gwen's team in Los Angeles in the Qualification Semi-Finals; killed by a Blue Candidate in the Qualification Semi-Finals; her death has a major effect on Gwen who feels partially responsible since she tipped the hoverboard of the Blue girl who fell to her death but whose rifle went off and killed Sarah; Gwen takes Sarah's body to the Huntington Gardens (an appropriate and respectful location to leave her body); Gwen also associates Sarah with Sarah Barrett Moulton whose portrait "Pinkie" hangs in the Huntington; long, stringy red hair and freckles; British accent; appears in *Qualify*.

Saramana Zhar (SAH-RAH-MAH-NAH ZHAH-R) – SPC Command Pilot of War-9; primarily Qurartu officers and crew; killed on board War-9 as it leaves Septu Station and is destroyed at the last moment by the golden light spheres of the alien grid; appears in *Survive*.

Sarpanit Latao (SAHR-PAH-NEET LAH-TAH-OH) – Games Contender, Blue Scientist Category; popular celebrity Scientist Contender who first obtains the Red Grail; in a melee, Gwen accidentally pulls Sarpanit's pants down and grabs the Red Grail, which Gwen immediately gives up to Deneb Gratu; killed by Deneb Gratu during Red Stage One; small-boned, deceptively fragile-looking, short, wavy gilded hair, river-red clay skin, dark, penetrating eyes; appears in *Win*.

Selmiris Teth* (SEHL-MEE-REES TEH-TH) – SPC Command Pilot of War-5; stationed around Atlantis; officers and crew primarily Crown Fleet from Vai Naat; escorts Princess Manala Kassiopei in the first *astroctadra* mission; escorts Princess Sheolaat Heru to Rah in the second Helios system *astroctadra* mission; mentioned in *Survive*.

Semiram* (SEH-MEE-RAHM) – ancient classical poet; author of *The Semiram Cycle*, ancient epic written during the Original Colony period, primary collection of myths about Arleana, Starlight Sorceress; nothing is known about Semiram who may not be an actual person but just an oral tradition of poets; mentioned in *Survive*, appears in the prequel series ***Dawn of the Atlantis Grail***.

Semmi* (SEHM-MEE) – ancient young scribe in the service of Arlenari Kassiopei whose writings are found on ancient scrolls; may or may not be associated with Semiram; mentioned in *Survive*, appears in the prequel series ***Dawn of the Atlantis Grail***.

Set – Trans-dimensional entity; golden being of pure light; takes on humanoid form with many arms to communicate with humans; ancient enemy of Atlantis; terminates the destructive OSIRIS program and grants peace to humanity when Gwen demonstrates the ability to use Starlight; appears in *Survive*.

Sheolaat Heru (SHEH-OH-LAH-AHT HEH-ROO) – Crown Princess and Heir of New Deshret; niece of the Pharikon (daughter of his deceased younger brother); has Logos Voice and participates in final Helios system *astroctadra* mission on War-5 at Rah; pleasant, deep alto voice; appears in *Survive*.

Shesep (SHEH-SEHP) – owner and proprietor of "Shesep's Bar and Fire Shawab" in Fish Town, Anu's favorite restaurant; serves *dea* meal to Gwen and her friends during Bride Show Day; stocky, middle-aged man with balding gilded hair, beefy hands; mentioned in *Win*, appears in *Survive*.

Shirahtet Kuruam (SHEE-RAKH-TEHT KUH-RUH-AHM) – First Priest of the cult of Kassiopei; Imperial loyalist and crony; in charge of keeping and recording all secret information about the Kassiopei Dynasty; advises the Imperator and Aeson in various aspects of their duties; IEC Member; political position: keep everything secret from the public, for as long as possible; Kuruam is a prominent noble family; older middle-aged, with a clean shaven skull except for one gilded forelock (symbol of his sect) running to the back of the head into a long segmented tail; leathery red-clay skin, unreadable dark eyes; mentioned in *Win*, *Aeson: Blue*, appears in *Survive*, *Aeson: Black*.

Shontae Smith – Candidate and Section Fourteen Leader, Yellow Quadrant Dorm, USA Team 14 at the NQC; older, brown-skinned teen with a do-rag on his head; appears in *Qualify*.

Siduaz (SEE-DOO-AHZ) – see Valel Siduaz.

Sofia Veforoi (SOH-FEE-AH VEH-FOH-ROY) – Games Contender, White Vocalist Category; specialty: opera singer, coloratura soprano; member of Team Kukkait; by Hedj's request, helps Team Lark with voice commands when Gwen loses her voice in Green Stage Three; finalist in the Vocalist Category tiebreaker; disagrees with Fawzi Boto's dispute of the results and gracefully concedes victory to Gwen; wish for land purchase on behalf of her impoverished extended family, east of the Great Nacarat Plateau, granted by Gwen; voluptuous, black wavy hair, brown eyes; beautiful, clear soprano voice; appears in *Win, Survive*.

Suval Denu (SOO-VAH-L DEH-NOO), Consul – see Major Characters.

Suval "Suvi" Gordon Kassiopei (SOO-VAH-L "SOO-VEE" [GORDON] KAH-SEE-OH-PAY) – second son and third child of Gwen and Aeson; Imperial Prince; twin brother of Romhutat Charles; three and a half Atlantean years old; mentioned in *Survive*, will appear in future books.

T

Tahirah Zulei* (TAH-HEE-RAH ZOO-LEH-EE) – Command Pilot of Imperial Command Ship Three (ICS-3) in the Earth Mission Fleet; aligned with the Red Quadrant; mentioned in *Compete*.

Takhat (TAH-KHA-T) – IEC Council Member, Imperial crony; political position: keep everything secret from the public, for as long as possible; votes on issues in tandem with the Imperator; witnesses the battle of War-8 and the alien enemy, followed by destruction of Tammuz Station by the golden spheres of the alien light grid; mentioned in *Win*, appears in *Survive*.

Tamira Bedut (TAH-MEE-RAH BEH-DOOT) – Arbiter (lawyer) who specializes in personal rights and Citizenship cases; high-powered city Arbiter highly recommended by Erita Qwas; Dawn Williams and Blayne Dubois meet with her before she is hired to represent Gwen in legal matters concerning her Citizenship; was formerly in a romantic relationship with Erita, now her ex-girlfriend; dances with Dawn at the Imperial Wedding, with a hint of romance to come; tall, full-figured, hazel-green astute eyes, strong features, shoulder-length wavy, naturally blond hair; sharp expression; mentioned in *Win*; appears in *Survive*.

Tammuz Akten (TAHM-MOOZ AKH-TEHN), Dame – Member of the Imperial Executive Council, Reform Faction of IEC; political position: Atlantis should comply with the aliens' demands, meanwhile, quickly select and train the best Earth Cadets for Star Pilot Corps duty; middle-aged, severe dark hair; appears in *Win, Survive*.

Thalassa (THAH-LAHS-SAH) – see Tiamat Irtiu.

The man in the golden mask – see "Rim, The."

Thebet Obwai (THEH-BEHT OHB-WAH-EE) – steward of the estate at Phoinios Heights; Aeson's old servant; wrinkled old man, onyx-black eyes, weathered red-clay skin, undyed dark hair turning grey; appears in *Win, Survive*.

Theresa – Candidate assigned to Yellow Quadrant Dorm Eight at the Pennsylvania RQC-3; student from Gwen's school in her first Agility Training class; appears in *Qualify*.

The Rim – see "Rim, The."

Therutat Nuudri (THEH-ROO-TAH-T NOO-OOD-REE) – The First Priestess of Amrevet-Ra (Deity of Love); commonly referred to as "The Venerable One;" oversees all high ceremonial matters regarding Imperial nuptials; in charge of the Bride during the Wedding events and preparations; officiates the Wedding Ceremony together with the First Priest of Amrevet-Ra, Darumet Azai; tiny old woman; mostly white hair with a few gold streaks in a bun, dark, sunken eyes; doll-like and terrifying; firm voice; appears in *Survive*.

Thoth – Trans-dimensional entity; golden being of pure light; takes on humanoid form with many arms to communicate with humans; ancient enemy of Atlantis; terminates the destructive OSIRIS program and grants peace to humanity when Gwen demonstrates the ability to use Starlight; appears in *Survive*.

Tiago Guu (TEE-AH-GOH GOO-OO) – Atlantean media personality; goes by "Tiago;" Host of *Grail Games Daily*, a popular entertainment show dedicated to the Games that interviews Contenders, profiles, analyzes, and covers the Games of the Atlantis Grail; one of the experts Aeson recruits to help train Gwen for the Games; being a former Games Champion himself, teaches Gwen strategy and the importance of motives in the Games; Buhaat Hippeis's media rival; interviews Gwen before the Games, then Gwen and Aeson together as a couple after the Games, as part of pre-Wedding media coverage; immensely wide, rotund belly, many chins, white-toothed grin; wiry gilded hair so short he appears bald; lapis-tinted brows; resembles a big, black, Laughing Buddha; rich baritone voice; clever satiated cat expression; wise and grounded; flamboyant dresser; appears in *Win, Survive*.

Tiamat Irtiu (TEE-AH-MAHT IHR-TEE-OO) – Games Contender, Green Entertainer Category; specialty: courtesan, martial artist, dancer, acrobat; nicknamed "Thalassa" or "blue sea" for her flowing, blue-tinted hair and amazing blue eyes; popular celebrity Green Entertainer since the Pre-Games Trials; retrieves the Green Grail in Green Stage Three; trussed up in a razor-sharp net, and her shoelaces tied together by Gwen; kills Zaap by shooting him from behind during the Triathlon Race in Yellow Stage Four; killed by Kokayi Jeet (who inherits her huge number of AG Points) to protect Gwen and as retribution for her killing Zaap; beautiful, vicious, petite; appears in *Win*; mentioned in *Survive*.

Tiliar Vahad (TEE-LEE-AHR VAH-HAH-D) – see Major Characters.

Tirinea "Tiri" Fuorai (TEE-REE-NEH-AH "TEE-REE" FOO-OH-RAH-EE) – Lady of House Fuorai of the Eastern Vadat Province and Eastern Quzakat Province, 127th generation, High Court; favored and vetted by the Imperator to become the future Imperial Bride and Consort of his son Aeson; House Fuorai is extremely wealthy and considered one of the most desirable connections in High Court; often calls Aeson via interstellar; walks in the Palace gardens with her girl posse; Aeson passes by her and instead picks Gwen as his Bride; rude and dismissive of other ladies and Gwen's friends, until Gwen dismisses her at the Ladies of the Court Bridal event; has to apologize to all those she wronged at the Imperial Wedding; tall, perfectly beautiful, doll-like, green-gold-hazel eyes, delicate arching brows, long, flowing gold hair, translucent white skin; superior, arrogant, petulant, selfish, bored; mentioned in *Qualify* (not by name), appears in *Compete, Win, Survive, Aeson: Black*.

Tremaine Walters – Candidate assigned to Yellow Quadrant Dorm Eight at the Pennsylvania RQC-3; during the first Combat class, asks about Aeson's black armband; ranks #2,985 at RQC-3, going into the Qualification Semi-Finals; assigned to Team USA 14C at the NQC in Qualification Finals; Gwen's friend; attends Gwen's secret birthday party at the NQC; can't swim very well but whistles sailor tunes when working with nets and cords; African American, skinny, with long locks; appears in *Qualify*.

Trey Smith – Qualified Candidate assigned to Green Quadrant, Brake and Shields, Cadet Deck Three Barracks on ICS-2; member of terrorist group Terra Patria; dates Brie Walton (who secretly agitates him and others in Terra Patria to participate in the hostile takeover of the Atlantean Command Ships, on orders of Earth Union); threatens Gwen's life, hits her on the head, giving her a concussion; shot and killed with a needle gun by Aeson in the Cadet Deck Four Meal Hall on ICS-2 during the hostage incident; alpha bully with a chip on his shoulder; tall, muscular, wavy brown hair, arrogant expression; appears in *Compete*.

Tuar Momet (Too-AHR Moh-MEH-T) – Games Contender, Red Athlete Category; specialty: weightlifter; joins Team Lark during Blue Stage Two; motive for entry in the Games: to receive an Imperial pardon for committing a mercy killing of his terminally-ill employer (at the man's own request) who sponsored his athletics and paid for his son's future; gravely injured as a result of being bitten and torn by *tif-nu-sha* during Green Stage Three, and unable to continue in the Games; Disqualified; fully restored to health by means of advanced medical care funded by Aeson; hired by Aeson to be Gwen's primary personal guard; receives full pardon for the *amrev seki* (mercy killing) as the result of Gwen's Champion Wishes on his behalf; tall, big, muscular, deeply tanned skin, hazel eyes, black hair in a long, segmented tail; appears in *Win, Survive*.

Tutanamat Argosaen (Too-TAH-NAH-MAHT AHR-GOH-SAH-EHN) – Lord of House Argosaen; husband of Irumala Argosaen; father of Devora; Aeson's maternal grandfather; hard of hearing but refuses to get his hearing fixed; called "Tuta" by his wife; introduced to Gwen at the Wedding; mild-mannered, handsome, elderly man, rich reddish-brown hair threaded with silver; soft, warm smile; appears in *Survive*.

U

Ujaste Naat (Oo-JAH-STEH NAH-AHT) – Games Contender, Blue Technician Category; specialty: tech gadgets; popular celebrity Contender, considered the most skilled Technician this year, famous as "Master of Gadgets;" assumes Favorite Kill status when Oshaharat Feveh (Drone Master) dies in Red Stage One; Team Naat inadvertently does something to the Blue Grail's round containment stone on top of the pyramid that releases hallucinogens over the pyramid; Ujaste and his entire Team Naat go into a panic under the influence of the hallucinogens, then fall or jump to their deaths, ending up as bodies underneath the pyramid, during Blue Stage Two; bland-looking, average build and height, short gilded hair; appears in *Win*.

Ukou Dwetat (Oo-KOH-oo DWEH-TAH-T) – Games Contender, Red Athlete Category; completely unknown Contender, comes out of nowhere to win the Category vacated by Celebrity Contender Deneb Gratu's death which opened the way for any of the lesser Contenders to step in; Games Champion #9; 3,428 AG Points; has been living homeless on the streets in abysmal poverty; Champion Wishes: permanent housing with a large vegetable garden for himself and his two young brothers; large, athletic, dark-skinned, short, curly gilded hair; appears in *Win, Survive*.

Uru Onophris (OO-ROO OH-NOH-FREES) – SPC Command Pilot of War-6; stationed around Atlantis; crew primarily Helios Fleet from Ptahleon; escorts First Speaker Anen Qur of Ubasti in the first *astroctadra* mission; escorts Princess Manala Kassiopei to the Helios system final *astroctadra* mission coordinates; after War-6 is destroyed by a plasma jet ejected from the star Helios, ends up marooned in space in the damaged *depet* together with Manala, Xelio, Consul Denu, George and others; rescued together with the rest by Aeson and Gwen using Starlight; appears in *Survive*.

Uxmal (OOKS-MAL), *Ter* – Imperial fashion designer who designed Gwen's four-layer wedding dress; appears in *Survive*.

V

Vahiz Fuorai (VAH-HEEZ FOO-OH-RAH-EE) – First Lady of House Fuorai of the Eastern Vadat Province and Eastern Quzakat Province; 126th generation, High Court; Lady Tiri's mother; introduced to Gwen at the Ladies of the Court Bridal event; bears a family resemblance to Tiri, gilded hair in a severe bun; haughty, cool expression; appears in *Survive*.

Valel Siduaz (VAH-LEHL SEE-DOO-AHZ) – elite PRT unit Captain in the SPC Special Forces; captain's call sign: "Imeier 1;" PRT unit's call sign: "Onyx (followed by personnel number);" assigned to Gwen's *Pegasei* Retrieval Team (PRT) on the *Pegasei* Retrieval Khenneb Mission, on board an *ankhurat*; young, medium-height, deep bronze skin, short black hair, black eyes; curt, no-nonsense manner; appears in *Survive*.

Vazara Hotat (VAH-ZAH-RAH HOH-TAHT) – Atlantean crew member aligned with the Green Quadrant, Brake and Shields, Command Deck Three on board ICS-2; friend of Gennio; offers friendship and fashion help to Gwen; a little too "girly" for Gwen; acts as the Music Mage (mysterious "sexy siren" voice, specially amplified, used to announce changes in gravity during a zero gravity dance) at the Blue and Yellow Zero-G Dances; petite, very slender, curvy hourglass figure, porcelain-rosy skin, pixie-like features, heart-shaped face, short gilded hair in a blunt cut; sweet, high voice; appears in *Compete*.

Vidam (VEE-DAH-M) – Games Contender, Yellow Artist Category; member of Team Gratu during Red Stage One; gambles with Gwen for a meal bar, is overcome by means of her hand piercing trick which gains her respect with Team Gratu and gets her the meal bar; works with Gwen and Kateb to use the water-filled drinking grails to create sound and disable the drone army; killed by Hedj Kukkait during Red Stage One when Hedj storms their Safe Base and kidnaps Gwen; large, bald-headed, covered in tattoos; appears in *Win*.

W

Wade Ruthers – Candidate assigned to Yellow Quadrant Dorm Eight at the Pennsylvania RQC-3, member of Team USA 14 during Qualification Finals, letter assignment unknown; alpha bully who engages in "hashtagging" Blayne Dubois; bullies Gwen; Olivia flirts with him; big muscular jock, dark blond hair, thick neck; appears in *Qualify*.

Wilem Paeh (WEE-LEHM PAH-EH) – the Crown Hereret (ruler) of Vai Naat; VIP guest invited to attend the Imperial Wedding; along with other heads of state, disputes the feasibility of *pegasei* liberation with Arion; older man, brown hair, light brown skin; appears in *Survive*.

William Windsor* – King of England; is aware (together with many other Earth leaders in the United Nations) of the stealth ark-ship AS-1999 in orbit around Earth; mentioned in *Survive*.

X

Xelio Vekahat (K-SEH-lee-oh VEH-kah-HAH-T) or (ZEH-lee-oh) – see Major Characters.

Xilith Keigeri* (KSEE-lee-th KAY-GEH-ree) – First Lady of House Keigeri; wife of Desher Keigeri, Oalla's mother; deceased; died just before Oalla started Fleet Cadet School; mentioned in *Aeson: Blue*.

Xofati (KSOH-FAH-TEE) – Games Contender, White Vocalist category; member of Team Gratu during Red Stage One; wants Gwen (her Category rival) to be dead, doesn't want any team resources wasted on her, thinks Gwen is a "useless privileged fool from a backward old world;" killed in a melee by a Team Latao Entertainer during Red Stage One; tall, curvy, gilded hair in a braided bun, intense unblinking eyes, dark and suspicious; appears in *Win*.

Xurut Ralafu (KSOO-ROOT RAH-LAH-FOO) – SPC Pilot assigned (along with Axela Buiri) as crew to Gwen and Oalla's *khepri* on the first *astroctadra* mission, their team headed to Mar-Yan; slim, olive-skinned young man with brown hair; appears in *Survive*.

Y

Yana Svoboda – Czech teen girl from Prague; mixed martial arts expert; one of six *shirén* Cadet Pilots assigned to Gwen's final PRT unit on the *Pegasei* Retrieval Khenneb Mission; short, stocky, blonde, blue-eyed; appears in *Survive*.

Yeraz Nuletat (YEH-RAHZ NOO-LEH-TAH-T) – Kateb Nuletat's wife who is unable to sing and form musical notes necessary to operate various modern technology, and is considered disabled by the Atlantean societal norms; Kateb enters the Games in order to be permitted to patent a device he invented to help her in that regard; attends Kokayi's Parade in Sky Tangle City and the Imperial Wedding; tall, slim, with long gilded hair; lovely, kind, expressive eyes, luminous expression; mentioned in *Win*, appears in *Survive*.

Z

Zaap Guvai (ZAH-AHP GOO-VAH-EE) – Games Contender, Green Animal Handler Category; the first Contender to join Team Lark, after Gwen trips him in the beginning of Red Stage One; mistakenly called "Zap" by Gwen; motive for entry in the Games: to purchase land in the Northern Sesemet Province to create a nature preserve for various animals; tells Avaneh and Tuar to never let Gwen see them peeing on the pyramid stones; first person on Team Lark to liberate and harness his *pegasus* from its orb; first of any Contender to ride his *pegasus*; tells Gwen "we'll work together now, no lies," and "I'll kill you later" until in the end he tells her she is his friend; killed by Thalassa during the Triathlon Race at the end of Yellow Stage Four; Gwen fulfills his posthumous wishes, buying the land preserve and naming it "Guvai," to be untouched by human hand, to allow the wild *sesemet* to roam free; skinny, wiry, quick, young teen boy, bronze skin, curly brown, barely gilded hair, dark eyes, cool and unreadable; appears in *Win*, mentioned in *Survive*.

Zabrodov (Pavel Matveyevich)* – Russian President; is aware (together with many other Earth leaders in the United Nations) of the stealth ark-ship AS-1999 in orbit around Earth; mentioned in *Survive*.

Zoe Blatt – Candidate aligned with the Yellow Quadrant; during Qualification Semi-Finals, Gwen Lark (with Sarah Thornwald and Jared Holder) commandeers her hoverboard in Los Angeles, and they agree to work together as a team; cheek grazed by bullet; gets to keep dead Sarah's Green Quadrant Weapon armor vest; assigned to Section 39 at the NQC; attends Gwen's stealth birthday party at the NQC; skinny, frail-looking, young; stubborn set of her angular jaw, brave blue eyes, light brown bangs; appears in *Qualify*.

Zua Kainaat (ZOO-ah KAH-EE-NAH-aht) – Lady of House Kainaat; 55th generation, High Court; part of Lady Tiri's posse at the Imperial Palace gardens; at the Ladies of the Court Bridal event, carries around a plate of appetizers for Lady Tiri until Gwen takes it away (plate gets passed around to everyone; Tiri tells Erita to hold it; Oalla takes it from Erita and drops it on the floor at Tiri's feet); approves of Gwen dismissing Lady Tiri at the Ladies of the Court Bridal event; at the Wedding, Gwen orders Lady Tiri to apologize to Lady Zua (and others); softly rounded face, pale blue eyes, river-red clay skin; mild, benign tone; appears in *Win, Survive*.

Various unnamed staff at Phoinios Heights estate
Various unnamed palace staff
Various unnamed *astra daimon*
Various unnamed Pilots in the SPC
Various unnamed members of the IEC
Various unnamed SPC Special Forces Members
Various unnamed Earth refugees, students, etc.

If You Enjoyed Exploring
PEOPLE OF THE ATLANTIS GRAIL
You are a Superfan!

Want to start the journey from the beginning?
*Catch up with your **free** copy of **QUALIFY**,*
book one of The Atlantis Grail!

*More **TAG novellas** and **novels** coming soon,*
including the 5th full-length TAG novel!

*But first—a new **prequel series** exploring the events*
of Ancient Atlantis, 12,500 years ago, begins in:

EOS (Dawn of the Atlantis Grail, Book One)
Coming soon!

While you wait . . . for a change of pace, try the intensely romantic historical epic fantasy **Cobweb Bride** . . . or the madly hilarious **Vampires are from Venus, Werewolves are from Mars**.

Don't miss another book by Vera Nazarian!
Subscribe to the mailing list to be notified when the next books by Vera Nazarian are available.
We promise not to spam you or chit-chat, only make occasional book release and news announcements.

Want to talk about it with other fans? Join the fun at . . .
The Atlantis Grail Fan Discussion Forum

About the Author

Vera Nazarian is a two-time Nebula Award® Finalist, a Dragon Award 2018 Finalist, and a member of Science Fiction and Fantasy Writers Association. As a double refugee, after emigrating from the USSR during the Cold War, and then escaping from the Civil War in Lebanon (by way of Greece), she immigrated to the USA as a kid, sold her first story at 17, and has been published in numerous anthologies and magazines, honorably mentioned in Year's Best volumes, and translated into eight languages.

Vera made her novelist debut with the critically acclaimed *Dreams of the Compass Rose,* followed by *Lords of Rainbow.* Her novella *The Clock King and the Queen of the Hourglass* made the 2005 Locus Recommended Reading List. Her debut collection *Salt of the Air* contains the 2007 Nebula Award-nominated "The Story of Love." Recent work includes the 2008 Nebula Finalist novella *The Duke in His Castle,* science fiction collection *After the Sundial* (2010), *The Perpetual Calendar of Inspiration* (2010), three Jane Austen parodies, *Mansfield Park and Mummies* (2009), *Northanger Abbey and Angels and Dragons* (2010), and *Pride and Platypus: Mr. Darcy's Dreadful Secret* (2012), all part of her *Supernatural Jane Austen Series*, a parody of self-help and supernatural relationships advice, *Vampires are from Venus, Werewolves are from Mars: A Comprehensive Guide to Attracting Supernatural Love* (2012), *Cobweb Bride Trilogy* (2013), and the four books in the bestselling international cross-genre phenomenon series *The Atlantis Grail*, now optioned for development as a feature film and/or TV series, *Qualify* (2014), *Compete* (2015), *Win* (2017), and *Survive* (2020).

After many years in Los Angeles, Vera now lives in a small town in Vermont. She uses her Armenian sense of humor and her Russian sense of suffering to bake conflicted pirozhki and make art.

In addition to being a writer, philosopher, and award-winning artist, she is also the publisher of Norilana Books.

 Get on my **Insider Mailing List**!
https://www.veranazarian.com/signup.html

Official website:
http://www.veranazarian.com/

 **Patreon** (Adult 18+):
https://www.patreon.com/VeraNazarian

The Atlantis Grail Fan Discussion Forum:
http://atlantisgrail.proboards.com/

 **Astra Daimon and Shoelace Girls** (Facebook fan group):
https://www.facebook.com/groups/adasg/

The Atlantis Grail – SPOILERS (Facebook fan group):
https://www.facebook.com/groups/tag2spoilers/

 **TAG official website**:
http://www.theatlantisgrail.com/

TAG Fandom website:
http://www.tag.fan

 **Norilana Books**:
http://www.norilana.com/

 **Facebook Author Page**:
http://www.facebook.com/VeraNazarian/

Twitter:
http://twitter.com/Norilana

 **Facebook TAG Page**:
https://www.facebook.com/AtlantisGrail/

Instagram:
https://www.instagram.com/vera_nazarian/

 **YouTube Channel**:
https://www.youtube.com/veranazarian-tag/

TikTok:
https://www.tiktok.com/@veranazarian

 **Goodreads**:

http://www.goodreads.com/author/show/186145.Vera_Nazarian

LibraryThing:
http://www.librarything.com/author/nazarianvera

 **Wattpad**:
http://www.wattpad.com/user/VeraNazarian

Linktree
https://linktr.ee/VeraNazarian

Blogs:
http://www.inspiredus.com/
http://urbangirlvermont.blogspot.com/
http://norilana.livejournal.com/

Acknowledgments

There are so many of you whose unwavering, loving support helped me bring this book to life. My gratitude is boundless, and I thank you with all my heart!

First, my immense gratitude to the incredible *astra daimon* and superfan Nancy Huett, who once again did the heavy lifting and compiled a comprehensive list of every character in the books. Same goes for the amazing Liz Logotheti and brilliant Shelley Bruce whose fact checking and number crunching skills kept me sane, and the almighty tech goddess Teri N. Sears whose technical wizardry brought order to the social media forums chaos. A special profound thanks to the wonderful Chris Marble for immense and timely support, going above and beyond, during complicated times.

To my absolutely brilliant first readers, advisors, topic experts, editors, proofreaders, fandom moderators, TAG Con Committee members and friends, Elizabeth Logotheti, Ellen Jauregui Contard, Harriet Bennett, Heather Dryer, Jeanne Miller, Kerry Vosswinkel, Mary C. Sellar, Nancy Huett, Nydia Fernandez Burdick, Ricki Bristow, Roby James, Shelley Bruce, Susan Franzblau, Teri N. Sears, and West Yarbrough McDonough.

To the lovely and wonderful group of Vermont writers and friends, Anne Stuart, Ellen Jareckie, Lina Gimble, and Valerie Gillen, and to my dear friends in more distant places, Lisa Silverthorne and Patricia Duffy Novak.

To all the wonderful and enthusiastic members of the "Astra Daimon and Shoelace Girls" Facebook group, "The Atlantis Grail – SPOILERS" Facebook group, and the official TAG Discussion Forum on ProBoards.

To my awesome and fabulous Wattpad friends and fans who keep re-reading each TAG preview chapter and making me smile, laugh, and otherwise delight in your hilarious, stunning, amazing, and insightful responses to the story! Thank you immensely!

To my new Patreon supporters, thank you, one and all, from the bottom of my heart, you are the absolute best!

If I've forgotten or missed anyone, the fault is mine; please know that I love and appreciate you all.

Finally, I would like to thank all of you dear reader friends, who decided to take my hand and step into my world of **The Atlantis Grail**.

My deepest thanks to all for your support!

Before you go, you are kindly invited to leave a **review of this book**!

Reviews are a wonderful way to help the author! They are also an exciting opportunity to share your honest thoughts with other readers, so **please post yours**, in as many places as possible!